Michael knew he must see Lora again . . .

Her face was radiant for so brief a time he wondered if his desire to see this response could have conjured it into awareness. "Perhaps it's for the best that you got this summons."

"Don't say that! I have to see you when you get back. I want you to get to know my children and my mother. And I want to meet your mother and sister."

He had been drawing her closer until her cheek was against his, but she remained there for only a moment. "I'd like to meet your family, Michael," she admitted, "but it's probably best for both of us if that doesn't take place."

He tried convincing her but she was immovable . . . . For that matter much of what he'd tried had not gone well.

EILEEN M. BERGER is an award-winning author with over 100 articles, short stories, and poems published in popular periodicals. Her inspirational romance novels, *Lexi's Nature* and *Tori's Masquerade*, and her biblical novel, *The Samaritan Woman*, established her as an important Christian writer.

Books by Eileen M. Berger

ROMANCE READER—TWO BOOKS IN ONE

RR3—Lexi's Nature & Tori's Masquerade

Escort
Homeward

Eileen M. Berger

Heartsong Presents

ISBN 1-55748-364-7

ESCORT HOMEWARD

PRINTED IN U.S.A.

one

Lora finished attaching the bar with its rotator and two lollipop lights to the top of her pickup. As she fastened the "Oversize Load" sign to the back, she heard footsteps coming around the long flat-bed trailer parked behind her with its mammoth, plastic-covered load. She turned and raised her arm in greeting. "So we're together again, Tony."

The middle-aged driver of the Peterbilt tractor cab spoke heartily. "I'm looking forward to it." Glancing back at a craggily handsome man following him, he said, "Michael, Lora Donnavan. And don't underestimate her 'cause she looks like that. She's smart and gets us through anything."

She tightened the final wing nut and walked toward them, her Reeboks almost soundless on the macadam of the huge mid-Pennsylvania industrial complex. "I'm pleased to meet you, Michael," she said, shaking his hand then turning toward Tony. "But I'm not sure I want to know what 'looks like that' refers to."

The stocky, broad-chested man drawled, "You'd prefer my rhapsodizing about your dark-haired, blue-eyed, slender, graceful beauty?"

She shook her head then warned Michael, "As you see, my friend tends to exaggerate."

The younger man's brown eyes crinkled slightly at the corners and his smile showed even white teeth that contrasted pleasantly with his sun-darkened skin. "Incidentally, my last name's Harrington."

Her eyebrows and voice raised in surprise. "Tony, I bet

you knew all along! Michael's the owner and manager of our truck escorting service."

Tony nodded and Michael seemed to be choosing words carefully as he shifted his weight from the left to right foot and slid his hands into his jeans pockets. "I need to ask a favor, Lora. It's been much too long since I've been on a run and I like to get out and experience what it's like for our escorts. Could I go with you on this trip?"

Wrinkles creased her forehead. She knew of only one reason why managers accompanied their employees. . . . "Have there been complaints about me or my work?" She didn't know what they could be, but perhaps some driver had been dissatisfied.

"Of course not! It's because of the good job you're doing that I chose to go with you."

She was flattered, but that didn't mean she wanted him with her. She needed this time by herself. She had been home for five days and had been incredibly relieved when this assignment came.

Her head remained slightly cocked as Michael went on. "If I don't go right away I won't be able to. And you are leaving this morning." He reminded her more of a small boy than a boss as he persisted. "Please, Lora, may I ride with you?"

"Do you have any idea what being together on the road for a minimum of six days could be like? And if I am lucky I'll get to escort another load from Minneapolis to somewhere else, so you could get stuck out there."

"I know."

Of course he did; he was the one to get the assignments for his employees, she thought foolishly. "Almost all that time will be spent either in my Nissan or in a truck stop," she went on.

His gaze did not leave hers. "I realize that."

She was beginning to lose hope of changing his mind but she had to try. "There's rarely time for sightseeing or stopping off along the way, and no matter how infuriated you might get with me or how much you'd want to take the wheel, I would be the driver and your primary companion. And the one with responsibility."

"That's understood." His honey-brown eyes looked directly into her blue ones. "You make it sound like I'm the one making the decision, Lora. I know I want to go with you. May I?"

"It is . . . irregular." She breathed out sharply, then shrugged, resenting not being able to refuse him. "You're my boss."

He shook his head as though at a troubling mosquito. "It's your truck, Lora. And your decision."

She knew she wasn't handling this gracefully even as she stood straight, her chin tilted upward. "And you can continue making my work enjoyable. Or miserable."

Sadness, perhaps pain, crossed his expressive face and then he unexpectedly smiled, apparently accepting her response as a refusal. "I promise I won't hold this against you."

She felt guilty somehow, and yet she so needed this time alone. She was annoyed that his being gracious about it made a difference in the way she felt. His open, friendly smile made her wonder if being alone in her cab for days with this very good-looking man could further endanger her fragile emotional state.

But that was not a valid reason to hesitate. She looked around at derricks and front-loaders moving unidentifiable metal constructions and at workers in hard hats walking around or directing activities. "Since I've always traveled alone, there's no way of knowing whether this could work," she said. Her eyes searched his and saw only sincerity. "I suppose we could try."

He held out his square right hand and, with only slight hesitation, Lora placed her slender one in his to seal the agreement. Maybe she wouldn't regret this, but she had the fleeting thought that she would feel more secure about the whole thing if she could forget the warmth of his hand enfolding hers in his strong grip.

Lora rubbed her open hand against a denim-covered hip. She and Tony discussed the instructions received from his company and the routing from here to the major highway outside of Edison City. Even though the load was extra-sized, measurements showed she would not need to fasten the "tickle bar" to her Nissan in the event of low-lying electric wires, tree limbs, or underpasses.

Tony tossed Michael the luggage that lay slumped against the front tire of the white cab then climbed in, taking charge of the entourage. "Let's get on the road."

Lora opened the cab's rear window. "Put your bag here, Michael," she suggested. Locking the window, she walked around to open her door. She seated herself then turned to bring first her right then left slim, jeans-clad leg under the wheel.

She leaned across to unlock the passenger door and gathered her maps, Bible, and two books from the seat and placed them inside the leather case she always took with her.

As she and Michael fastened their seat belts, there was a slamming of doors and roar of engines, and she eased forward until the other truck was directly behind her. They went through the gates, stopping long enough for Tony to hand the guard authorization for taking the massive load from these premises.

Lora glanced toward Michael while they waited for a sufficiently long traffic break so both could cross. She had not looked at him before, partly because of the importance of what she was doing but even more because of her persistent awareness of his being there. Was that the faint scent of aftershave? *Probably my imagination*, she thought.

"I'm always grateful once we're on a main road," she commented, feeling compelled to say something. "Back-street maneuvering can be stressful."

He nodded but said nothing and she pulled forward, keeping an eye on her mirrors to make sure Tony was with her. A difficult right-angled turn a little later was at a traffic light. Even though the other vehicle required the full width of intersecting streets, they managed to get through.

Her shoulders relaxed against the sturdy gold fabric matching the truck's exterior. "From here on it should be relatively simple."

Michael spoke for the first time since they left the plant. "This brings back some of the tensions of this job."

She was watching what the mirrors reflected almost as much as the ascending curved ramp in front of her. "I didn't realize until today that you had escorting experience. You should let us know that."

"I doubt it would make a difference."

It did for her. "A lot of people think going all over the country is like a permanent vacation. It's good that you know what's involved."

"Somehow you," he emphasized the word, "always sound as though you're having a great time. For that matter, my dispatcher and I both reach for the phone when we think it could be you."

His smile looked genuine. "Is that why you're both so

pleasant when I make end-of-the-day reports?"

"Could be. With some drivers, all we get are complaints."

Despite the compliment, she felt she should remind him of her breakdown last week.

"I know, but you also told of a puppy's antics outside the phone booth and the rippling gold of wheat fields."

A brief silence hung between them. "That must be boring when you're not there to see it, but . . . I do appreciate pets and growing things."

"And mountains and oceans and boats on the Mississippi," he added.

She had not realized how often she did this. "I must seem awfully unprofessional."

He looked startled. Turning toward her, he laid his left hand on her arm. "Don't change. Please. We look forward to your calls."

Normally she would not have given further explanation but now she did. "All the time I was growing up and even when getting my degree I never had the opportunity to travel or go anywhere. Now I'm a child in a toy store, permitted to play with anything. Everywhere I go there are such marvelous things! Even when traveling the same roads, the seasons have changed or the play of clouds is intriguing." Motioning toward the fields on their right, she deliberately caused him to remove his hand even though, no, because, she rather liked having it there.

"I, we appreciate your sharing these things with us, Lora." He was looking straight ahead. "By the end of the day we often need something upbeat."

She gave him a quick glance. "And I'm it?"

He grinned at her. "You're an important 'it.' Betty and I thank you."

The silence between them then was hardly noticeable because of constant chatter on the CB. "There are times I'd like to turn it off," Lora said, reaching to reduce the volume when a particularly offensive message was given. "But there's always the chance that the next information could make a difference in how or where we're going."

He nodded and she asked, "Remember my getting held up for several hours in Indiana six or eight weeks ago? The accident blocking the highway was far enough away that I might have been able to get us rerouted had someone notified us in time. As it was, we got stuck between exits."

His thumb motioned over his left shoulder. "No way of getting that turned around, even if you wanted to."

She heard her name and answered immediately. "How's it going, Tony?"

"Fine back here. But how 'bout speeding a bit going down this hill?"

"If you speed up, my friend, I undoubtedly will. I'm not about to get squashed."

"And your buddy up there? Will he fire you if you go too fast?"

"I'll check." She looked toward him with raised brows. "Will you?"

Michael looked uncomfortable. "That's a no-win question. If I say it's okay, I encourage breaking the law; if I forbid it, I'm an ogre."

She was enjoying this. "So?"

"I'm . . . pretending you didn't ask."

Lora was already picking up speed. "Coward!"

"Sometimes I practice expediency," he confessed.

"Or hoping problems will go away?"

"Or resolving not to read the speedometer. . . ."

They did not stop for lunch but Lora insisted Michael get sandwiches and cans of soda from the cooler for both of them. "Do you prefer bologna or ham?"

"I don't want to eat yours," he protested again.

She answered matter-of-factly. "You might as well. The extra is in case there's a long delay of some sort. We'll eat our major meal at the truck stop where we hole up for the night."

After Michael made the call-in back to Pennsylvania, they stopped for the day in Ohio. This was the first time she had not made the call herself, but Michael needed to check on office matters so she relayed information through him. Learning she had no messages, she left to carry her bag to Room 104. It wasn't long before Tony strolled down the hallway. "Ready for food?"

"Just about." Lora brushed the short, dark-brown curls away from her face and paused in the act of closing her door. "Perhaps we should call Michael . . . ?" But then she pulled it tight and walked beside Tony. "He didn't say what his plans were, but he'll find us if he chooses."

"Things didn't go well with you two?" he asked with what sounded like sympathy.

She hadn't thought of it that way. "Not bad. We talked mostly about the scenery and driving, things like that."

"Is he married?"

She laughingly nudged his arm. "I've been alone with him in a truck cab for most of the day and don't even know that. He does have two kids, so presumably they have or had a mother. He didn't volunteer personal information and I didn't ask."

They walked into the large, bright room sporting the strangest assortment of pictures, antique farm tools, and animal heads she could imagine. She veered away from the booth directly across from the door. "I have no objection to looking at a moose while eating, but I don't appreciate one leaning over me."

She raised her arm on seeing Michael in the doorway and he came toward them with a diffident smile. "I should have asked earlier. May I join you?"

"Of course." She slid along the red plastic seat, making room for him. "We usually assume we're eating together unless told differently," she explained, then looked up as the waitress handed each of them a menu and asked if they'd like coffee.

By the time their hot drinks arrived the hungry trio was ready to order. Steaks for the men and a seafood platter for Lora were placed in brisk fashion.

It must be my fault we didn't talk more in the truck, Lora decided as she half-listened to their conversation while finishing her meal with pie. She enjoyed and contributed to their discussions of world events, the state of the economy in general and trucking in particular, and a brief recounting of the time each had spent on the road.

Baseball, however, was something else completely. She'd understood her father had liked the sport, but she had only vague remembrances of his sitting or lying on the couch in front of the TV set. After all, she wasn't quite five when he was killed.

She could recall how distraught her mother was at receiving the news. Sally, eighteen years older than Lora, had made some statement like, "Well, Mom, at least now you know where he is." Years passed before Lora realized her father had been an alcoholic who, though an excellent carpenter, was often on binges and usually with other women on weekends.

Tony's voice roused her. "Hey, dreamer, pass the sugar."

He must have asked for it before. "Sorry," she said, handing him the two-compartment container of sugar and artificial sweetener. "I was thinking of something else."

"Obviously. And it wasn't necessarily happy."

He probably meant that as an invitation to share her sober thoughts, but this wasn't the time or place for confidences, even if she'd consider speaking of personal matters.

When she did not respond, they reverted to the merits and problems of the teams they'd been considering when last she'd paid attention. She couldn't have been woolgathering too long.

They paid their bills and Michael glanced at his watch. "Anyone wishing to join me for TV is welcome."

Tony was silent until Lora said, "You're here on the lower level, too, aren't you, Michael? Well, sure, let's do that."

Tony, apparently reacting to her obviously including him, went along. An hour later when he started to leave Michael's room for the built-in sleeper in his cab, she left also, stating she wanted to get back to the fascinating Simon Brett mystery she had brought with her.

While still at breakfast the next morning, Lora and Tony again reviewed the routes they'd be taking and they were off ahead of their schedule.

Michael looked at the perfect profile of the young woman. Had he guessed wrong in deciding to ride with her? She'd seemed so delightful and outgoing on the phone but was reserved in the truck beside him. He'd started conversations on many topics and she appeared willing to discuss them, sometimes adding more insights and observations than he'd expected. But she had introduced few subjects since right after they'd started out.

He had learned early on not to ask questions answerable with yes or no, or he would receive no more. He cleared his throat. "How do you fill your free time, Lora?"

Did she hesitate? She gave a little sigh, he was sure of that. Was she annoyed at his bothering her? "I have little free time. When I do, or take it, my most frequent recreation is reading. Mysteries, historical fiction, romances. Sally calls it my escape-from-reality fix."

"Who is Sally?"

"My sister. Single. Also living at home."

He was surprised. "You live with your parents?"

This time he knew she paused and he hoped he hadn't pushed too much. He was relieved when she answered, "My father died in an automobile accident when I was little. My sister has a physical problem, so she's there with Mother. Besides, I need a place to call home between runs."

The way she said it, almost in a monotone and not looking his way, made him realize he'd gone as far as he should along this line. He couldn't bear to go back to silence. "You mentioned a mystery writer last night. Is he your favorite?"

He had offered another yes/no question but this time got away with it. "Simon Brett? He's very good. But my last book was by Ngaio Marsh and, before that, P. D. James. Every so often I go on an Agatha Christie binge or reread one of 'The Day the Rabbi Did Thus-and-so' novels."

He wished he could converse about these but the only one of these authors he'd even heard of was Agatha Christie. "How about nonsedentary activities?"

She shifted on her seat and her hands changed position on the wheel. "I used to be on a volleyball team, and was good at it. But my schedule is so erratic I gave that up. And I haven't bowled for years."

That would probably be before she came to work for him, but he had not determined a way of wording an additional question before the CB squawked and Tony was saying he'd like to pull off at the rest stop coming up.

Lora put on her turn signals immediately, but also sent the message to Tony about the white eighteen-wheeler that had been crowding her for the last ten miles and was now beginning to swerve left around them. Because of his load, there was no way even with extra mirrors that Tony could see what was taking place directly behind him.

Michael and Lora got out as soon as they parked and stretched muscles cramped from being in the Nissan. Tony opened his door and turned to sit sideways on the high seat. "You two can go in first and I'll follow," he suggested.

Lora shook her head. "This was your idea, so the honor's yours."

Tony grinned, jumped down, and headed for the long, low building. "Keep an eye out, kids."

Michael asked, "Am I missing something? Yesterday we all went at once."

Lora frowned as her gaze slowly circled the heavily wooded area behind the facilities. "Earlier today a big white truck—I didn't think it significant at the time and didn't mark down its company or license number—came up and rode too close to Tony for too long.

"And that Banning Transport one that just passed didn't get off my tail even when we changed speed a half-dozen times after I signaled Tony. It is probably a coincidence, but it's safer to stand watch."

He must be slipping. "What signals do you use? I didn't notice a thing."

"You weren't supposed to." She smiled as though thanking him for a compliment. "Only once that I know of have my signals been vital to the safety of a load, but I always have something worked out that the driver's sure to catch but isn't likely to be recognized by others."

She hadn't answered his question, but he had to give grudging admiration. He had better sense, however, than to tell her that. "Do you know what the load is that you're escorting?"

She shook her head. "I don't want to. All I know is we take something big from Pennsylvania to Minneapolis and turn it over to the assigned person. And then I hope to pick up another load somewhere in that vicinity and go on."

They did not speak much after that as it seemed expedient to circle the vehicles slowly, but in opposite directions. Tony got back soon and said, "Run along, you two. I'll watch things here."

Michael matched his steps to Lora's until they parted outside the building. She apologized when she returned. "I'm sorry it took so long. There was a line . . ."

"No problem. I just arrived." Actually, more time had elapsed than expected, but he'd stood there, hands in his pockets, looking around. Waiting for her. He was totally unprepared for the pleasure he felt when she came quickly, gracefully, toward him along this unremarkable gray cement sidewalk at a typical rest area in the western part of Indiana.

Had there been more to his decision to travel with her than he'd admitted to himself? Was his smile too eager, too boyish? He hoped not, for he was sure she wouldn't welcome his being anything more than a one-time traveling companion.

She still didn't appear as friendly in the truck as on the phone. Did the long-distance element give her more security? Did she dislike him in person?

She walked in front of him between a van and car parked along the curb and had turned to hear what he was saying when Tony shouted, "Lora! Watch out!"

Michael saw a beat-up old Ford truck backing from its spot a split second before she did and his left arm shot out to encircle her, to pull her back against himself. His eyes narrowed and stomach tightened at the sharp pain along the back of his forearm from a torn piece of metal sticking out.

His first concern was for her. "Are you all right?"

Her face was white, but her voice steady. "Yes." When she saw his arm, bright red was pouring from the gash and dripping on the ground. "Oh, my dear, you're really hurt."

She couldn't realize how she'd addressed him but he hugged the words to himself. Drawing tissues from her pocket, she pressed them on the wound. "Hold these on tight and come with me."

Tony ran toward them, but she waved him back. Michael tried to tell her he was okay, but she guided him to her truck, opened the passenger door, and insisted he sit down. She left him for only a moment, returning with a remarkably well-fitted medical case.

Peeling the plastic covering from sterile four-by-fours, she wet the gauze with an antiseptic lotion. He had to consciously keep from wincing as she cleaned the area. Tony assisted by unwrapping several more of the square bandages that Lora laid on the cut with instructions to Michael to again press down firmly.

She kept up a running commentary about what she was doing and which things would or would not hurt and he watched her intent face as she ripped open a package of tape strips. She lifted his hand from the compress and her blue eyes were still dark with concern as they looked up at him.

"The cut isn't as long as I suspected and probably not as deep. However, it does gap and bleed a lot, which is good, of course, since the dirt and rust from that old truck should have got flushed out. I'm going to use these tapes to draw the sides of the wound together and hold them there. Like having stitches," she added.

As she finished, she asked, "Would you like me to drive you to a hospital emergency room?"

He looked at her with surprise. "What could they do that you haven't attended to?"

She sat back on her heels and ticked off items on the fingers of her left hand. "They could make you fill out lots of forms, let you sit in the waiting room for a long time, order blood work, put in stitches, and give you antibiotics." She raised the index finger of her right hand as she added one more item, "And present you with a sizeable bill."

"I think I'll pass!"

Her hands were gentle in applying a protecting, tape-held layer of gauze. "There is one important consideration, though. Do you remember when you last had a tetanus shot?"

He couldn't forget that. "Last August. I'd been working on some swimming pool plumbing and got a ragged cut on my hand."

"Good, that you got the shot, I mean. Otherwise you should have protection. But really, if you do want to go, I can leave Tony and take you to wherever that might be."

"No, thanks." Michael shook his head. "Let's be on our way. We've wasted enough time."

"Not exactly wasted," Tony drawled from where he was

leaning against the side of the gold Nissan. He had just walked around his truck again, even though he told them he thought the rusted vehicle that had injured Michael was driven by a very scared teenager.

Tony had written the license number and a description of the Ford and boy but Michael didn't want to be tied up making a report, even though he admitted to Lora he'd expect his employees to do so.

Lora repacked her kit and they were soon back on the road. Michael had hoped she'd continue talking as while caring for his arm, but that was not the case. He smiled though, remembering her concern. "That's quite a medical kit you have." He waited for a response that didn't come. "With your expertise and manner, you should be a nurse."

He thought she wasn't going to say anything this time either, but she finally, though reluctantly, did. "I am."

"Do our records show that? I don't remember seeing it." Michael's gaze traveled to Lora's hands, hands a moment ago that were a study in competency and efficiency. Now both hands were gripping the wheel so tightly the knuckles were white.

two

Lora could hardly believe she'd told him that! She was certainly not ashamed of her nursing degree and had worked hard to get it. "The information that I have my BS degree from Penn State is there. I did not indicate which discipline I'd chosen."

"Why not?"

She avoided looking at him but was aware he had turned as much as his shoulder strap would permit and was staring at her. "For the very reason you are curious now."

"Wouldn't you be if our roles were reversed?"

He sounded defensive and she sighed, feeling herself relax a little. Before answering, however, she reported to Tony the information that a "pack" of four trucks and a number of cars were bearing down on them and the left turn signal of the lead Chrysler had just been activated.

The roar of their passing made her raise her voice. "Of course I would wonder. Today's shortage of nurses makes it possible for us to pretty well call the shots as to where we want to go or what we want to do."

He said nothing so she added, "The salary's much higher than what I make driving my truck, which I must buy and pay expenses for. Even when I go directly from delivering one load to picking up another I don't do as well financially, and I pay my own health insurance and have no sick or vacation days. . . ." She'd heard these arguments so often Lora thought she sounded like her sister!

"So?" he nudged when she didn't continue.

She resented his making her go into this part of her past, but she had allowed the door to be opened. "I've wanted to be a nurse for as long as I can remember, and I've always loved children. It was only natural that I would choose pediatric nursing. I've even worked in a pediatric intensive care unit."

Lora had seldom spoken of this to anyone and doing it now hurt almost too much. Could she get away with her line about always wanting to travel and now having the opportunity of being paid for doing what she'd almost be willing to do free?

But Michael's interest seemed genuine and she sensed he wouldn't be judgmental. "I was good at my job," she finally managed, her voice strained. "And I loved it. Perhaps too much, I don't know." There was another long silence. "I came to love each and every one of my little ones."

"Wasn't it good to love them?" he asked gently.

The fingers of her right hand pushed back roughly through her curls. She had asked herself this so many times. "I was under the head nurse at first, so she had responsibility for things. But it wasn't long before I was given charge of the second shift. And the third baby who came on my first evening died within an hour of his arrival. The next week another died. Though I'd done everything possible . . ."

Michael wondered if he should hand her a tissue from the box in front of him but she seemed unaware of tears sliding down her finely boned cheeks. His natural instinct would have been to lay his hand on her arm in an effort to comfort, but he feared she might brush it off or stop talking. He silently prayed for wisdom and remained where he was, barely breathing.

"I stayed on," she finally said. "For two more years. I thought it would get better, and perhaps it might have if I just could have had some time free from having to. . . ." She bit her lip and fumbled with her right hand for the Kleenex.

Michael held out the box and she withdrew several, one after another, rubbing rather than blotting her face. "I'm sorry, Michael. I haven't cried once since I came to work for you, and that's been over a year."

He no longer controlled the impulse to touch her. His hand squeezed her arm firmly as he said, "Lora, my . . . friend." He'd almost said my dear, as she had so unconsciously before. "Don't apologize for tears. God gave them for a purpose, I'm convinced of that. Maybe they'll help you feel a little better about things."

He felt a little shiver passing through her. "That first baby had only been sick, really sick, for a matter of hours. Nobody had any idea it was viral encephalitis until too late."

"And the second?" He did not know if it were good or not to pursue this, but it felt right.

She stared straight ahead. "We were told by the mother and her live-in boyfriend that little Terry had fallen from his high chair and that's how he broke his arm and leg. But when I touched him, he cried. I remember brushing back the hair from his forehead and kissing him and . . . he screamed."

She swallowed hard. "I suggested we needed further checking and, oh, Michael! He lost consciousness before the bone scan was taken. A new skull fracture was revealed along with some partially healed ones. And three cracked ribs and a broken right thigh bone just beginning to heal."

Michael felt half-ill himself from hearing this and thinking of his own two children he loved so much. He remained silent as her low voice continued. "We realized he had internal bleeding and gave him blood and attempted emergency surgery to remove his ruptured spleen. . . ."

There were no tears now, only her eyes narrowed and face set with pain. "His whole six months of life must have been horrible, undeserved, unending agony! And then he died. In my unit. . . ."

"Oh, Lora, how awful!" He couldn't have told whether he had more sympathy for the baby or Lora at that moment. His arms ached with the need to embrace and comfort her as she had doubtless done for her charges. But she was behind the wheel.

They must have traveled a mile before she murmured, "And there were so many others. . . ."

"And you helped most of them." He was sure of that.

"Yes." She nodded slowly. "I have nothing to regret as far as that is concerned. But there were too many times when, though giving all my professional skill and encouragement and love, it made no difference in the outcome."

Her full lips pressed together in a straight line. "I suppose you want to know what it was that made me quit, walk away."

It was a question, even though there was no inflection at the end of the words. He wanted to know desperately but was saved from having to voice this when she went on, bitterness directed against herself, not him. "There was a three year old, Tanya. She had a form of leukemia that responded to none of the treatments, although her parents took her to the best- known, finest institutions in the country.

"She was brought to us several times during crises and we pulled her through." Lora drew in a deep breath through parted lips. Looking out the rearview mirror abstractedly, she continued.

"And there was our happy little Manny who, at four, was

in the process of dying from AIDS. He had never known his parents, but the couple who took him into their home did everything possible for him. He was in no way deprived. Except of health. And a future.

"And," she finally looked toward him, her feelings nakedly revealed. "I couldn't handle the prospect of being there when these children I loved so much would die."

Michael's hand slid upward and kneaded her tense, knotted shoulders. "There's no way I could handle that, Lora."

"But I'm a nurse." It was a cry of agony.

"Before that, more than that, you were a feeling, loving woman." *What a wonderful friend, or mother, she would be*, he thought admiringly. "There's a limit to how much a person like you could be expected to bear." He told of reading that a large percentage of employees in intensive care or other high-stress areas in hospitals could only continue this a few years. He then asked if she'd considered transferring to another department.

"Of course I thought of it. I even requested going to obstetrics or to the extended care facility where I figured I could serve well even though, perhaps because, they are such different disciplines. But there were no vacancies in a supervisory capacity in either place and the nursing office and personnel insisted I was too valuable to do floor nursing!"

"So you resigned," he said, trying to help.

"And so I left." The words could have meant the same but her connotation was that of failure instead of transition. "I answered an ad in the paper for a temporary job as an escort for a mobile home company and made my first run for Harbinger Homes the day after my three-week notice was fulfilled at the hospital."

She reported to Tony information about the traffic behind

them before going on, "After a few months I decided I'd like to drive long-distance or cross-country, so I went to a truck stop and talked with some escorts. Several of the most contented drivers were working for you, so I applied there."

The corners of her mouth turned up a little as she glanced toward him. "And the rest is history."

He was incredibly relieved that she could smile even that much right then. "Or the present," he offered as a possible correction.

"Or the present," she repeated after him.

They bought prewrapped sandwiches and cold sodas at the truck stop where they stopped for gasoline. It would be impossible to arrive in Minneapolis before the highway department's curfew but they continued as long as possible and stayed over at a place Lora remembered from another trip.

She was not surprised when Tony announced, "I'll be sleeping in my truck again tonight. You guys go get your accommodations."

"Not for me, Tony," Lora stated. "I'll be in my Nissan parked right here beside you."

He did not argue. She knew he'd never have asked this of her but he was honest enough to admit he'd be glad for her presence.

Lora tossed her keys to Michael with the suggestion he get his gear from the truck, but he carried them back, placed them in her hand, and folded her fingers around them. "If you're staying here, Lora, so am I."

The sudden warmth in her cheeks made her feel like a schoolgirl. "Thanks anyway, Michael, but you don't have to," she protested. "I always bring my sleeping bag with me, and this isn't unusual."

"You shouldn't sleep in your truck."

He seemed genuinely concerned, perhaps from fear he'd be held accountable if anything happening to her. "Ordinarily I do this only when coming back from escorting, not when I'm on the job for you," she explained. "And I've never had any untoward incidents.

"As for tonight, neither Tony nor I believe those white trucks and the rusty one were more than coincidences, but we'll sleep better not worrying about what could be going on out here."

He again insisted while they ate together and as bedtime approached that she should not be sleeping in the truck. If she did, he wanted to be there with her.

"Look, Lora," he said finally, "if you're afraid of what others will think or say, I'll reluctantly agree to getting a room. However, if it's that you don't trust me to behave myself, I swear I will. For that matter, I saw that you have a whistle and mace. It's okay with me if you wear the one and tuck the other inside your sleeping bag."

She knew that under the bright light where they'd parked he could clearly see the blush that now for a second time was burning her face. How she hated her inability to control that! "It's not that I don't trust you, it's just. . . ." She hesitated before finishing. "I really want you to go to the motel." To avoid looking at him right then, she climbed into the truck to unpack the air mattress.

She had not expected him to be so helpful. He followed her in and was the one to blow up the flat plastic. He didn't even seem breathless as he placed it out of the pole light's direct glare and unrolled her sleeping bag on it. "There you are, my lady."

The sweep of his arm was truncated and his bow was from a squatting position but the effect was strangely charming. She knew she had been right in insisting that he not sleep here.

"Please reconsider, Lora," he pleaded one last time. "I'd do fine here with just your extra blanket." His palm pressed against the medium-pile brown carpeting that covered padding on the floor. "This is softer than the ground last Saturday night when my kids coaxed me into sleeping with them in the backyard tent."

"Sounds like they know how to get their way with you," she said ruefully.

He laughed easily. "I'm afraid they do. But they're neat kids."

She backed out the short distance on hands and knees and he followed, bumping his head on the cap. "There are times when a van would be an advantage," she commented, then rushed in more words so he wouldn't misunderstand. "There's not much headroom for me, at five-eight, and you're appreciably taller."

He seemed totally relaxed and comfortable as they headed for the restaurant. The brilliant lighting of the area made his face as easy to read as though it were daytime. Knowing this would be true for her as well, she resolved to keep from revealing more of herself. "Tell me about your children," she said as they took milk shakes into the "Truckers Only" lounge a few minutes later.

His chuckle was warm and friendly. "I give you fair warning: Proud fathers are every bit as biased as those proverbial grandmothers."

She slid into a comfortable chair near the wall, indicating her readiness to learn about them. His knee bumped against hers as he twisted to get the soft leather wallet from his hip pocket. She didn't want to embarrass him by moving away, but on the other hand, she didn't mind the contact. She was conscious of the spot he had touched even after he shifted position to extend the opened picture section toward her.

"She's beautiful," Lora said, looking at the candid shot of the black-haired, brown-eyed five year old poised to jump from a diving board into a large, blue-tiled pool.

"And not only in appearance," he added, his voice softened with love. "Abbie has a delightful disposition almost all the time, though I'll admit she does have her moments."

"I'm glad she's human, not Saint Abigail."

"Oh, she's quite human. In every way." There was a slight pause as his thumb moved across the plastic in an obvious caress. "I'm overconscious of how well she's doing. She was only two when Chrissie died from a ruptured aneurism in her brain that we never even knew she had. And Chuck was one year old at the time. I don't know how we'd have managed if my mother hadn't come to stay with us."

His eyes were still focused on the picture of the laughing child, but his mind was on the past. "Abbie had a rough time that first year, with nightmares every night and crying spells and clinging to Mom and me. But," he straightened his shoulders, "she's doing great now. And Chuck," extending the likeness of his stockily built, blond four year old, "is just—Chuck."

She laughed and he grinned and shrugged broad shoulders. "There's no easy way to describe Chuck for he's a bit of everything. He's a chatterbox, yet eagerly wants you to tell him the whys and hows of the universe. He takes apart toys or anything else—nothing's safe, actually—but he's not destructive by nature, it's just that he needs to know what makes things work.

"He's bright, too, but not doing as well in preschool as his sister did, probably because he's daydreaming or talking when he's supposed to be listening and doing things."

"What about his attention span?"

"Incredible, with things that interest him. Not long ago we visited an uncle's farm for a week. All day, every day, he was feeding chickens or currying horses or petting kittens or building dams or catching crayfish in the little stream, completely content and happy. And, in the process, keeping his sister busy, for she's not as good at entertaining herself."

He continued speaking of them, needing only a few comments from Lora for encouragement. But one question that she most wanted answered she couldn't ask. *What had he meant when he said he must make this trip now or not at all?*

Later, they went back out together and climbed up into the cab to talk with Tony, contentedly ensconced in the sleeper behind the cab's seats. He lay propped up in his extralong bed reading *The New York Times.* "Almost ready to call it a night?" Michael asked.

"Not quite." Tony shook his head and shifted his sock-clad feet. "There's rarely a problem with security at a truck stop, but there are no guarantees, either. I talked to a state trooper inside who said they drive through on a regular basis, but we drivers sorta look out for one another. I'll make another round or two before I try sleeping."

"And you probably plan to be up a number of times during the night," Lora said. "How about taking turns setting alarms so we'll both sleep more soundly when we have the chance?"

The smile directed at her showed appreciation and

fondness, but he spoke to Michael. "Like I said before, this one's all right. I'd recommend you keep her."

"I hope to," he said emphatically. "For a long time."

Was there more to Michael's response than just words? Lora wondered excitedly. "I'm serious, Tony," she said. "I'm doing the checks at twelve, two, and four, and you go between those times."

Michael leaned forward to stare at her. "If you think you're coming out here to check on goodness-knows-what while I'm sleeping in the motel, you're out of your mind! I am going to stay with you in the truck and go with you on your rounds."

"No, Michael, you're not. It is my truck, and, as was established from the beginning, I'm the one to make decisions as to what's done on this trip!" she flashed back.

Tony interrupted, "Just as this is my responsibility, which I'll see to. It's good having you nearby, Lora, on the remote chance I'd need you to call someone, but I want both of you to sleep. . . ."

Lora felt caught in the middle but knew what she had to do. "It's up to you, Tony, if you want to get up at twelve, two, and four." She turned away and slid down to the ground. "However, if you do, I'll see you then, which would be rather stupid. I am going to be checking at those times. I've already set my watch for twelve and I am not changing it."

"Stubborn woman!" Tony exploded, but Michael saw the grudging smile he was trying to hide. "Try talking some sense into her, will you?"

Michael looked after the young woman rapidly traversing the distance to the building. Eyebrows raised quizzically, he asked, "And what do you think are the odds of my succeeding?"

Tony sat up and put his folded paper on one of the built-in shelves. "So what am I supposed to do?"

"Well, if I were you I'd enjoy sleeping through twelve, two, and four. I promise she won't be alone then, even if she won't permit me to sleep in the truck."

She appeared almost angry when he was waiting for her at midnight, but he said mildly, "Lora, we can stay here and argue or go make rounds so we can get more sleep. However, since you're going, so am I."

Frowning, she hopped to the ground from the back and started around the rear of the rig. He hurried along the right side, passing her at the far left corner of the cab before completing the circuit. "Shall we retrace our steps?" he asked when they met again near where they started.

She shook her head and, leaning down, flicked the beam from her powerful flashlight back and forth under the load and cab. She repeated this from the rear and far side also, making sure the large wheels offered no blind spots.

Was she as fearless as she appeared or was she doing this in spite of fear? He suspected the latter.

She didn't speak as she climbed back into the truck. "Lora?" She turned to face him, her silence somehow shouting. He suggested, "Please sleep through the two o'clock circuit. I'll be here to make it."

This time she was angry. "Michael! Don't do this! I am the escort and choose to do it my way. You have no right to interfere."

He gave her a long look. "I'll go in, Lora, but I'll see you," he said glancing at his watch, "in one hour and thirty-nine minutes."

He'd slept comfortably until his alarm had awakened him, but now turned and tossed. He was still awake at one, but must have dropped off soon afterward. Nevertheless, he was at the truck as Lora came out and they repeated their check of two hours earlier.

He feared she wasn't going to say anything at all this time. Resolving to go along with that, he was unbelievably relieved when she said in a little voice as she was ready to go back, "I'm sorry I was so rude, so ungrateful, Michael. I do appreciate what you're doing."

He was turned toward her, his face shielded from the bright light shining on the back of his head. He suspected she could not see his smile, but he couldn't have kept it from his face. "It's all right, Lora."

"No, it's not. Not really." There were creases across her forehead and she was obviously finding this difficult. "I've never had a man want to help me, just to help me. I don't know how to act."

He wanted to reach across the short distance separating them, to hold her and assure her he wanted to be there for her. But he must not. "Just accept it, Lora. That's all I ask."

He could see her distinctly as she struggled with this. Finally she said, "I'll try. And now," beginning to climb inside, away from him, "I'd better let you try to sleep. It won't be long until I, er, we are up again."

"Good night, then, if that can be said under these conditions."

He heard her little chuckle. "Perhaps 'sleep quickly and well' would be better?"

"Very good. Sleep well, Lora."

"And you too, Michael."

He did not sleep well, but he wouldn't tell her that. Even so, he was not terribly drowsy when he met her at four. "Did you sleep?" he asked.

"Fairly well, thanks." She accepted his assistance in getting out of the truck and this time he policed the far side of the rig first. Their routine was now set and it wasn't long until they separated again. Even at this hour trucks arrived, filled up at the tanks, and left. Voices were heard offering greetings and farewells.

He wondered how alert he'd be in the morning, and it was suddenly that. The sun was not up yet but it was bright enough that the lights that had shone through the night had automatically been shut off. The day promised to be almost perfect.

He took his shower, got dressed quickly, and was almost to the truck when he saw her climb out. He stopped where he was, just watching. Her head tilted upward and she stretched, as unself-consciously as a kitten, rising onto her toes as her fingertips lifted toward the sky.

She relaxed then and her gaze slowly circled her restricted area bounded by Tony's truck and another diagonally parked. Michael started toward her, not wanting her to be embarrassed or annoyed at his seeing her like this. He was rewarded by her beautiful smile. "Michael!"

But then her feet, which had started to bring her toward him, came to a complete stop and her expression of welcome became more guarded.

"It's still early, Lora, but I woke up and thought I might as well get shaved and cleaned up."

"I hope you didn't come out this time to check the truck and me. Tony just made rounds."

He was close enough to reach out his hand, palm up. "I came to give you this."

She looked from the motel room key back up to his face, a concerned question in her eyes. He reassured, "I'm finished except for picking up my bag. There are lots of fresh towels and shampoo, and privacy. It will be a lot better for you to take your shower there than to wash up in a public washroom."

She hesitated for only a moment before reaching for the key. His hand automatically started to close around hers as her fingers touched his palm, but he controlled their movement. She said, almost formally, "Thank you for thinking of this."

They walked together around the load and met Tony on the far side. Lora said she would meet them for breakfast after her shower. It wouldn't take her more than the fifteen minutes they estimated it would require for them to check the oil and be ready to leave.

"I see you've already showered," Michael said, noting Tony's wet hair.

"That's one of the perks for me, Michael, a free shower if my tanks are filled at a truck stop."

Again this day they ordered substantial breakfasts and, while waiting for the waitress to bring them, Tony used the table-side phone to check with his company. He had a pickup about forty miles from where they'd be dropping their load.

"Wonderful!" Lora was obviously happy for him. "And now a question important to me: Is it something needing an escort?"

"You don't have a return run?"

She looked at Michael with raised brows. "As you know, the nearest option I had was for western Indiana. Okay for this if it works out?"

Michael knew she'd like going on with Tony. "I'd think so. I'll call as soon as we finish eating," he added as the waitress set his platter of ham, eggs, and home fries on the table. He noticed that Lora again had her hands in her lap and bowed her head briefly before eating.

Tony remained perfectly still during this and Michael rather guiltily gave a silent prayer of thanks also. Prayer was part of every meal with Mom and the kids, but he felt uncomfortable with a display of piety when not with them.

Betty was not yet in the office so he left his request on the answering machine that arrangements be made so Lora and he could get the run to Kansas City, if possible. He would verify this later.

Even though Lora took time to clean and rebandage Michael's injury, they were on their way earlier than expected. He commented, "We've certainly been blessed with wonderful weather."

"True, but I don't ordinarily mind rain and we're usually stopped before fog becomes too great a problem. Snow and ice are worse, especially in the Rockies. I've had several stressful runs there."

"I remember!" he said with feeling.

She looked at him from the corner of her eye. "I'm afraid you do, especially last January."

"I'm still convinced you should have followed my advice and refused to go on."

She was very serious now. "That was the closest I ever came to saying that. But the load was to meet a ship for India and we had to get there by the specified time."

He'd never forget that day. "Betty and I paced the floor and prayed until we finally got the call saying you'd made it."

Her hand left the wheel, moved slightly to the right, and grasped it again. For a moment he thought she was going to reach out to him. "Thanks for your concern. And for your prayers."

She shifted on the seat. "Betty . . . is the one who interviewed me for this job. I can see her knowing me well enough. . . ."

He wished her words had not faded away. "I'd come to feel I knew you at least enough to worry about you as an individual as well as an employee." He didn't want her to feel uncomfortable but yet he wanted desperately to get closer to her. If it took him from here to Pennsylvania, he would find a way to reach her.

three

The weather was perfect for July, not hot enough for putting on the air conditioner but too lovely to drive with the windows closed. The smell of the forests, the gold of ripening grain, and the rippling blues of the ever-changing sky fascinated Lora. On days like this she could drive forever.

Especially with this man beside her.

How had that treacherous thought found room within her consciousness? Her life did not have room for daydreams as potentially self-destructive as this. She decided to ask him the question she had wondered about since that first morning. "Michael, why did you say that if you didn't make your trip now you might not be able to?"

He rearranged his long legs, ending up this time with the right one straight, the left bent at the knee, heel against the front of the seat. "My mother has been staying with us for several years, as I told you. She's been wonderful in every way. She has a tremendous amount of patience and love and Abbie and Chuck adore her.

"About ten months ago she began dating a man she and Dad had been friends with for over thirty years. They're both widowed, Sam for two or three years, Mom for six. They began going to church together and concerts and then started singing together in the community chorus one night a week."

He had been opening a pack of hard candies and offered one to her. "I'm pleased about their growing closeness for they deserve and need one another. I wasn't surprised when they told me this weekend that they plan to marry soon and,

38

well, Sam has a lovely home on the other side of town where they'll be living."

She glanced over at him, realizing what must be coming. "Mom's bright-eyed, sparkling, and obviously looking forward to her new life and being with him, which is certainly right, but she also feels guilty about leaving us."

"What will you do?"

"Well, first of all, I want to get this run out of the way. . . ."

"Thanks!" She pretended insult at what could be taken as his desire to be finished with her company.

"You know that's not what I meant," he said sternly.

She flashed him a smile. "Sorry."

The corners of his mouth pulled downward as he shook his head in reproof. "My mother says she'll try to help when I really need her and I've already given up Rotary and most evening activities. A young woman from church who's at home with two little ones has even agreed to baby-sit."

"I'm glad." She was, incredibly.

"Things will work out."

Lora wasn't sure if she should ask what next came to mind. "Does . . . Chrissie's family have the children some weekends?"

"They originally asked for them every other one but," he hesitated as though deciding how to put this, "I don't plan on that. Perhaps one month they'll take them both times and then six weeks or more go by with only a phone call."

"Does this upset the children?"

"I don't think so. They do enjoy the time there as the folks usually have something exciting or special planned. Knowing the Tambours, I suspect they will have less interest in being with the kids as time goes on."

"I suppose that's inevitable."

"They became especially doting grandparents about a year ago when I was dating 'too seriously' and 'too soon,' as they put it."

From the corner of her eye Lora saw the candy wrapper being crushed by the involuntary tightening of his hand. She ached for him, and perhaps for herself as well. She reached to turn up the CB to pick up information from drivers coming toward them. Several told of a bad accident six or eight miles ahead. Then there were reports that ambulances were leaving the scene and clean-up was far enough along that one lane was open to traffic.

She spoke into her CB. "Tony, we could make a detour in a mile or two, but it sounds like there should be room for your width when we get to the accident scene. At least we shouldn't have to wait long. Okay with you if we keep going?"

"Sounds good to me, Mushroom."

Michael seemed more relaxed now on the seat beside her as he asked, "How did you choose Mushroom as your CB handle?"

She reset the cruise control after braking for a car pulling back in line. "At the time I was discouraged and somewhat depressed when I took what I expected to be only a short-term job as an escort. Nobody could understand why I'd made the change. . . ."

How well she remembered her sister's bitterness and anger that had driven her from the house that night! "I'd been trying to think of the right name—not too cutesy or obtuse—when I stopped at a steak house for dinner and big, fresh, delicious mushrooms were served with the meat.

"It suddenly struck me that no matter how black, rotten, or messy their surroundings, they continue growing and become the best they can be." She could feel his gaze fixed on her. "But were I making that decision today, it would be different. I no longer need that constant reminder."

When they got to the accident, officers guided Tony slowly past the mangled remains of two automobiles and gave them the good news that, although there were injuries, nobody appeared to be critically hurt.

She glanced at her watch. "Michael, would you please get out the routings again? I think I've memorized everything, but we offload near the western side of Minneapolis and don't get to use a bypass."

There was one turn requiring backing and filling and she wondered out loud what underpasses, wires, unsafe bridges, or hazards made the Department of Transportation send them through instead of around the city.

When they arrived, derricks removed the load from the rig and they were free until it was time to pick up their next one. A supervisor pointed down the street when asked about getting a good lunch. "I'd suggest Quentin's. The food's substantial and well seasoned. It is on your way, and there should be room to park."

It seemed strange that this was the first noon meal they had eaten together. Tony chewed a bite of his corned beef sandwich and washed it down with coffee. "Planning to ride with Lora for her entire trip, Michael?"

Lora straightened when she became aware she was leaning forward, eagerly awaiting his answer. "That depends on how long it is. I'll probably fly back. From somewhere."

She determined to not think about after he was gone, but she didn't totally succeed. She had liked being alone in the truck; would she now be lonely?

Later that day they picked up an immense turbine and

started for Missouri. They spoke of many things, mostly trivial, but on the following day he asked if she were dating anyone.

"Not . . . seriously."

"One man in particular?"

"Not now." She was a little surprised to realize she had hardly thought of any man other than Michael for days. She was watching the road ahead and keeping an eye on the heavy bank of clouds that fifteen minutes ago had appeared as little more than purplish haze on the horizon. She welcomed the opportunity for a change of topic. "The weatherman warned that this storm was moving rapidly, and we're heading right into it," she said. "Have you noticed most vehicles coming this way have their lights on?"

Lora soon found herself fighting the wind that swayed her truck and almost pushed them off the road. She turned the CB higher when the beating of the downpour on metal and glass drowned out most other sounds. "What do you think, Tony? Want me to pull off the highway?"

There was no hesitation. "Let's keep going, that is, if you can see well enough. Stay at this pace, nice and easy."

"There's probably more danger of someone piling into us if we're standing still," she agreed. "Anyway, you don't have to worry about being blown off the road with all your weight."

Tony's voice sounded plaintive. "You don't have to get personal."

"The load's weight, you clown!"

There was an audible sigh. "Oh, that's better. I was beginning to think you'd changed."

She suspected he was deliberately keeping the conversation light because of the brewing tempest, so she responded in kind. There was more banter until someone with the handle of "Wanderhund" came on, asking to meet Mushroom at the truck stop ahead. Lora's answer was crisp. "No, thanks."

"I could show you a good time," he coaxed. His voice dropped almost an octave into what he evidently regarded as inviting. "So whatchasay we meet up at the next stop?"

She gripped the steering wheel tightly but before she got any words out Tony cut in, "She's already taken, Wanderhund. Hands off."

"Are you?" Michael asked in the relative quietness of a lull in the rain and wind.

Did he still wonder if she were "taken," or if she might conceivably meet someone like this? She shuddered at the thought. "Even without the dangers of AIDS and other assorted diseases, I can't imagine going off with a stranger to a motel."

"Many do."

"And a lot of us don't!" she retorted. She turned on her left signal and gradually pulled toward the other lane as there were parked vehicles on the road's right shoulder. "But I do know of formerly upstanding people—female and male— who have messed up their lives that way," she admitted.

"It's all too easy when they're away from home. They feel accountable to nobody."

She nodded. "There are always people who are ready for anything. And titillating movies and VCRs seem to be available everywhere."

There was a short pause before Michael spoke, a more thoughtful tone in his voice. "One of the things I'm trying to find out is why there's so much attrition, why so many who seem to like escorting give it up."

Lora was glad for the change of topic. "Unfortunately, they're often the best, most trustworthy employees."

"Too frequently."

He seemed troubled by this; perhaps she could help. "Well, there are the young people just wanting to get away from home and do their own thing. Pretty soon they find it isn't as much fun as expected.

"Others get tired of being on the go all the time and unable to maintain a social life. Or they've been running away from something, then get it straightened out after experiencing what it's like on the road."

Tony was safely in her lane. "A woman I drove with three weeks ago had recently moved from North Carolina to upstate New York to be with the driver she'd traveled with six months before. She can't see that if he hasn't asked his wife for a divorce by now he's not going to. In the meantime, she's left her original service and signed on with another."

"And what makes new people keep coming?"

"That depends on the person," she said. "Basically, this is an unskilled job in that you don't need a college degree or expensive training. Kids just out of school and in love with cars may find it perfect for a while. The pay's not bad—for unskilled individuals—and for the most part you're pretty much your own boss.

"Also, housewives who've been tied to responsibilities may decide to try this once the children are grown, particularly if they don't have husbands."

"And the older men?"

She relaxed against the seat, reassured he wasn't using this to keep conversation going. "Most I've talked with are retired and use the extra money to supplement social security. In that case, they work only until reaching the allowed maximum.

"Also," she laughed suddenly, remembering, "two men I know always wanted trucks but were unable to persuade their wives. They've both got shiny new ones now, due to 'needing' them for escorting."

He smiled back at her, then sobered. "And you, Lora? What will make you leave?"

She had tried to avoid asking this of herself. "That hasn't happened yet."

His voice was soft. "But it will someday, won't it?"

She couldn't look into his face, afraid he might read too much from hers. "Probably. Someday. In the meantime, I'll take each day as it comes."

Michael wondered if she suspected the importance of his question. As owner and manager, it was well to know if an employee were unhappy and considering a change. In this case, however, her continuing employment might be the only way in which to keep in touch if he could not persuade her to see him socially. "Might you return to nursing?"

She waited so long he feared she wasn't going to answer. Should he withdraw the question? But there was something almost confessional about being alone in a vehicle with another person and things were frequently shared that would otherwise not be spoken.

"Not in pediatric intensive care. I'm positive of that."

It was stated with such finality that he kept quiet for the next twenty miles. The time was not wasted, however, for he went over in his mind what she had said during these days. He probably shouldn't have probed as he had but he'd have learned little about her otherwise.

There were major holes in her story. Why was she still living at home? It couldn't be just because it was less expensive than having a place of her own. Even had she not mentioned her early promotion to supervisor he'd have realized she was capable and could handle things well.

What kept her so busy she didn't have time for occasional bowling or volleyball if she enjoyed them? How involved had been her relationships with men? She hadn't seemed traumatized when indicating she wasn't dating seriously, but the only time she'd let go of her tightly reined emotions was in regard to children in her care at the hospital.

She seemed unaware of his scrutiny. One minute he had been trying to figure out what she was thinking, then, unexpectedly, he was wondering if she weren't the person he'd like to love and marry and have as a mother for Abbie and Chuck.

Thoughts like that had not been on his agenda. He had wanted nothing more from this trip than, as he had told her, to check on conditions his escorts were facing.

He now had something much bigger to think about. Michael considered himself a good salesperson when promoting his business, which had grown more rapidly than he'd dreamed it could. To sell himself and two active young children to this wonderful woman would undoubtedly be much more difficult.

Dear God, please help me . . . he silently prayed.

Why did this man have to pick her truck anyway? Why had she permitted this constant prying into her affairs? Did he do this to everyone he met? The average businessperson surely did not have time to become involved or interested in every employee.

And now he was just sitting there, staring at her. Well, she would jolly well ignore him and continue driving! If he were waiting for her to begin a conversation he would wait a long time.

It was Tony on the CB. "Hey, Mushroom. Foot stuck there?"

She looked at the speedometer and removed pressure from the gas pedal. "Sorry!"

His voice was cheerful. "I'm not, not really. It's just that you never, well, never mind."

She was mortified, yet grateful for his manner. "Thanks, Tony. I appreciate your calling me on this." She couldn't explain to him or anyone the anger, the perverse resentment she had been feeling toward the man sitting beside her. It had even made her break her own safety rules. *How could I let myself go like that?* she asked herself, but to Tony her voice was apologetic. "My mind was wandering, I'm afraid. It won't happen again."

He stayed on the CB only a little longer and then there was silence in the Nissan. Finally she said, "I suppose you'd like to know how fast I was going."

"No. I'd rather not."

She wanted to look at him but did not permit her gaze to leave the dark gray surface of the road with its apparently endless center stripe. "It was kind of Tony not to say what it was."

"He seems like a fine person."

Tony was a good safe subject. "He is. From what I've seen, I'd trust him anywhere, any time, and under any circumstances."

"He thinks a lot of you, also."

"I believe so. And he respects me. That's why I feel bad that he had to correct me."

"You make it sound like a reprimand from your father."

She didn't care if wistfulness did show in her voice. "I wish, if I could have chosen a father, he'd be a lot like the man in that truck."

What would life have been like had that been the case? For her and for Mom? And for Sally? What if he hadn't always drunk too much? And if he had been faithful? Maybe he wouldn't have been killed in that car and they could have had a more normal life.

It wouldn't have kept Sally from getting multiple sclerosis, of course, but the symptoms began about then. The diagnosis was made within a couple of years and Sally, pretty, pert, and popular, gave up hope of making it as an actress and came home for Mom to care for.

Lora had not thought of calling home for the past two days, but she would tonight.

She checked into her room and was walking with the men toward the dining area when she saw a woman come through the front door. "Go ahead and get a table," she said, her hand touching Tony's sleeve. "There's someone I want to talk to."

Tony grinned. "Bring him along if you want to. . . ."

She laughed and deliberately didn't tell which of the arrivals she was interested in. "Sure I will," she responded, then hurried across the open area. "Katie, Katie Bronson!" she cried, giving the midthirtyish woman a hug. "I never expected to see you here!"

There was almost a drawing back or away, yet Katie's voice and the expression on her face appeared as pleased as Lora's. "It's good to see you! I've thought of you often and . . . wished you were around."

Something was wrong, radically wrong. The pretty face was not as symmetrical as usual, and it wasn't just that the dark brown hair usually worn pulled back in a perfect French braid was now hanging down, almost straight. There was nothing Katie could do to make herself unattractive, but. . . .

With the tip of one finger Lora touched the right cheek below and in front of the temple. Katie winced, her eyelids flickering downward to cover the not-quite-clear brown eyes. Lora asked, "Ken? Again?"

Lora couldn't quite identify the expression in the eyes, a mixture of fear, agony, and perhaps even a little relief at seeing her friend. "Night before last. We've been separated now for six months and, and he's not allowed to come to my apartment, you know. But he did—drunk again—accusing me of awful things."

Lora reached for Katie's duffel bag and insisted on carrying it to her own room. Katie permitted herself to be brought in and seated on the foot of the nearest queen-size bed. "I appreciate your wanting to help, but Ken may be following me. I think he is. A shiny Ford truck looking like his has been staying about the same distance behind us all day."

Lora couldn't help glancing toward the door, wondering if the dead bolt worked. "Did you tell your driver?"

She shook her head. "He'd think me paranoid or something. Just like the police do." Her right hand, nails bitten to the quick, came up toward her lips.

Lora shifted a chair from beside the small round table to face Katie. Seating herself, she suggested, "Better fill me in on what's been happening."

She wished it were not so predictable, so pitiful. Katie and Ken had been married for fifteen years, the first third apparently not being too bad, or perhaps it was by comparison with what followed that Katie referred to them as "the good years."

Ken had always had a temper, but as time passed he kept it less under control. Especially with his wife. When he struck her the first time he was as horrified as she and promised it would never happen again. She thought he meant it; probably he did at the time. But he'd hit her again a month later and with increasing frequency since then.

When Lora helped her move last winter it was after Katie got the job with Champka Interstate Escort Service, as Lora's company didn't need anyone at the time. Lora even loaned her the first month's rent, security deposit, and enough to tide her over until she was paid for her first couple of runs.

Lora silently thanked God again that she'd been home in January when Ken beat Katie so badly. She took the battered woman directly to the emergency room and it was the doctors' documentation of cuts and bruises that made it possible to secure the court order to keep him away.

But now to have been severely injured the night before she started out on this run and then to have been followed! "Does he still have last year's four-wheel drive?"

"Oh, sure. He loves it, which is more than can be said about his feelings for me!"

Lora handed Katie the box of tissues and let her cry. She pondered the situation in her mind. If it is Ken, he knows Katie's truck as well as his own. What will he do when he learns she's not registered here?

Katie blew her nose again and started to get up. "I shouldn't be in your room. If he sees you're registered. . . ."

Lora motioned for her to remain seated. "They're computerized at the desk. There was no way I could have known who else was here, so he can't either. And we don't even know if it is him. You weren't close enough to actually see his face, were you?"

"But the truck looked like his, and stalking me like that on the highway is just the sort of thing he'd do." Her face and voice showed her apprehension.

Lora stood up and busied herself with taking toiletries from her bag and putting them on the dresser nearest the window. She also closed the curtains. "Katie, why should he have followed you here when he knows you'll be back in Pennsylvania after the run?"

"I don't know. Unless," her voice dropped almost to a whisper, "he plans to kill me."

"Katie!"

"Well, he might think he could accomplish it easier away from home."

A chill ran up Lora's back and she tucked her elbows tightly against her waist as she realized this was not beyond the realm of possibility. She must keep calm for both their sakes. "Somehow, as . . . impulsive as he is," she had almost used the word violent, "I'd think if he meant something that serious he'd have done it when he hurt your face."

The attempt at a smile was ineffectual. "My face got off easiest, Lora. You should see my back, shoulders, and hips."

Lora laced her fingers together and gripped her hands tightly to control their trembling. "Did you call the police?"

"I couldn't." The almost-straight hair flipped to the left then the right. "A neighbor did when she heard me screaming. It was the noise of the sirens that made him leave. Through a window onto the fire escape."

"If she hadn't . . . ?" She could not go on.

This time her hair moved forward then back. "I don't think

I'd be here today."

Lora took a deep breath. "Have you slept at all?"

"Very little. I've been too scared."

Lora reached to put a hand on her friend's shoulder but drew it back in time. She didn't want to risk pressure on an already bruised area. "Katie, go soak in a tub of hot water while I order food to be sent to the room. What would you like?"

"Nothing. But please, if you haven't eaten, go do so."

"I'd rather eat with you tonight."

Katie's eyes opened wider. "You were on your way there when I came, weren't you? Were you with others?"

Lora was grateful she hadn't been seen with the men as that would make Katie feel even more certain she was taking advantage of her friend. "Had I eaten with anyone, it would have been the driver out of Minneapolis. And I'd prefer being with you. So what would you like, a full-course dinner? Steak and fries? Pizza? Sandwiches?"

Katie was about to protest again but thought better of it. "A pizza would be fine, if you eat most of it. I don't have much appetite."

Lora refrained from mentioning that Katie had lost at least ten pounds. Instead, she reached to help her friend to her feet. "How about taking your pajamas or gown into the bathroom with you? I'll let you know when the pizza arrives."

Katie did as told and Lora phoned the request for food to be brought in a half-hour. She then called Tony in his cab to ask if he'd casually walk the parking lot to look for a one-year-old black, short-box truck with Penn State decals on the front and back and a small souvenir football hanging from the rearview mirror.

Stressing the necessity for caution, Lora asked if Tony

would call her back as soon as he made the rounds. Her hand remained on the phone for a short time before reluctantly letting go. There was no justifiable reason for her to call Michael about this situation. Wanting to talk with him, to share her concerns, was not enough.

She turned on the bedside lamp, picked up her mystery book, and propped herself up on extra pillows. However, she did not turn the pages. Replacing it on the stand, she reached for motel stationery and a pen from the drawer and began writing some of the things she knew Ken had done to Katie. She didn't know dates—there were other incidents which should be included—but this was a beginning.

She lifted the phone half-way into its first ring. Tony had found the truck parked eight down from Lora's. Had this been deliberate or a coincidence? Had he recognized the Nissan? "Tony, this man is really sick. I don't know what he's capable of."

"Are you in danger?" Tony's voice showed his worry.

"I don't think so, but my friend is. And I'm not sure how to protect her. It will help, though, if you'll go with us for breakfast, and also to our vehicles later."

"I'll be there. I promise. . . ."

She had time for little more than thanks because of the knock on the door. She opened it after checking through the little peephole, accepted and paid for the food and beverages, and carefully relocked the door before calling, "Let's eat while the pizza's hot!"

She immediately heard water going down the drain. She would not tell Katie of Ken's presence but, if she felt it wouldn't cause too much additional stress, she'd ask for dates and times of the things she'd written and also for additions.

She hoped there might be a good comedy on TV afterward to get Katie's mind off her problems. She hoped even more that they might get a good night's sleep, although she wondered if that were remotely possible.

four

Katie seemed almost drowsy by the time they ate so Lora didn't have the heart to ask any questions. Perhaps the poor woman would have a better chance of going to sleep early if they avoided speaking of problems. Hopefully they could record further information in the morning.

Lora wondered if she'd catnapped at all between the times Katie got out of bed, once to go to the bathroom then look through the peephole and the other to wander around the room and stand at the window looking out over the parking lot.

"Are you checking to see if Ken's truck is there?" she asked.

The silhouette shifted as Katie turned. "I wondered . . . yes, I was," she admitted. "I tried not to wake you."

Lora stretched to turn on the bedside lamp and patted the side of the bed in invitation for her friend to sit there. She pushed herself up toward the headboard and arranged pillows behind her shoulders. "Perhaps I should have told you before, but I wanted you to rest. Yes, Ken is here."

Katie's eyes were enormous in her terror-filled face. "How do you know that?"

Lora realized she feared Ken had made contact with her. "He has to know you're here, but I'm sure you're safe for the night," she said after telling of Tony's help. "What worries me most is how you can be protected once you leave here."

The slender, nail-bitten hands were gripping the legs of her cotton pajamas. "If he wouldn't obey the injunction against him in Pennsylvania, he certainly won't honor a court order here, or in the next state we come to. Or the one after that."

"That's how I see it too."

Katie's shoulders slumped, her hands sliding downward onto the bed. Her eyelids quivered as they partially closed, showing an acceptance of hopelessness. Through trembling lips she managed, "I might as well give up."

"Oh, no, you won't! Not after coming this far!" Lora leaned over to reach for the pages laid face down on the stand between the beds. "I started something while you were in the tub, but it needs your help. In fact, it's got to be your project if there's to be a chance of success. Willing to consider it?"

There was no hesitation. "If there's the remotest possibility of success, of course I am."

It was nearly three-thirty when they turned off the lights again. Lora struggled to keep awake until she was sure from the soft, regular breathing that her friend was asleep. She wished she had a lap-top computer, but the handwritten pages would have to suffice.

The alarm rang all too soon but Lora felt reasonably rested as she padded to the bathroom for a quick shower. She called Tony's truck to ask him to come earlier than planned and both women hurried to complete preparations for leaving.

Only at the last moment did she permit herself to phone Michael and was unprepared for the rush of pleasure in his voice. "And a good morning to you, Lora. What a great way to begin the day!"

She forced herself to go directly to the purpose of her call. "I, I wanted to tell you we're going to breakfast now."

A brief pause told her he was probably remembering their plan to eat half an hour later. "I'll meet you there shortly."

"Michael, I'm sorry." Her voice was little more than a

whisper and even she couldn't have said for sure which she was most sorry about: not calling earlier, or not telling him about Katie.

The warmth and depth of his voice reassured her troubled mind. "Are you all right?"

Her laugh sounded unconvincing even to herself, but she couldn't explain things with Katie in the room. "I'm fine."

"Is it your friend?"

He must have seen her greeting Katie and realized something was wrong. "We'll talk about it over breakfast. Tony just arrived."

As she hung up she turned to greet the driver, introduce Katie, and pick up her bag. By silent, mutual consent Katie was between them as they walked down the hallway, and Tony remained with Katie at their corner booth in the dining room when Lora said she was going to the desk to check out.

She took longer there than probably would have been expected, for the man on duty also made photocopies for her and permitted Lora to fax several of them. No matter what might happen to her or Katie, Lora felt others had to know what had preceded this day.

She had turned to start back to the dining area when she saw the tall, broad-shouldered man she'd been subconsciously looking for. Michael's concerned face lit with a warm smile. "I think I'll avoid any rush and get my finances taken care of now also."

She could not have moved away even had she wished to. He was so handsome, so real, so interested in everyone and everybody. "You meant it when you said you'd be here in a few minutes."

He set his bag in front of the counter and responded to her before turning toward the clerk. "I woke early and got showered and shaved. There was little to keep me." She waited with him as he slid his credit card from its plastic protector and paid for his lodging. Picking up the luggage with his left hand, his right one slipped beneath her elbow.

She looked up with a tilted smile. "I feel like a little old lady and you're an overgrown boy scout."

Small vertical creases appeared for a moment between his brows. "I can't think of any less apt description of you, Lora."

It would be all too easy to fall into companionable patter with this man, but she had little time to take care of more immediate concerns before joining Katie and Tony. "We have a major problem, Michael. My friend, Katie, was a battered wife. She's now legally separated and there's a Pennsylvania injunction barring Ken from hurting or from even being near her. But he's followed her, is here it turns out. We don't know what to expect."

She paused in the doorway, her eyes quickly checking each patron. "I was wondering, though. It may be best if you aren't seen with us."

"For my sake? Or hers?"

She drew in a quick breath. "I was thinking of yours, but I suppose for hers too. After all, with two men and two women eating breakfast in a motel dining room, it could be all too easy for an insanely jealous man to make wrong conclusions."

"Is he mentally ill?"

"He hasn't been declared so legally," she admitted, "but he's got to be, to do the things he's done. So there's no reason you have to get involved."

His arm slid around her shoulders. "We're in this together, Lora. All the way."

She did not immediately free herself from his embrace, as her willful thoughts chose to consider this. Although people in the restaurant must see them, her head rested for just a moment against the softness of his green T-shirt and she was conscious of the lub-dubbing of his heart against her cheek. Or was the pounding from her own unruly pulse?

Oh, God, help me! she prayed silently. *Don't let me fall in love with Michael. I can't handle more complications in my life.* She refused to acknowledge to herself that this request may have been made too late.

The waitress arrived as Lora was introducing Michael to Katie and the newcomers ordered without looking at a menu. Lora had expected the conversation to center around Katie's problems and was surprised at how relaxed she appeared now.

Lora caught a questioning look from Michael and, having no idea how to interpret what was going on, raised her brows and slightly moved her head sideways and back again.

Suddenly it hit her: Katie expected to die! As in those last minutes or hours before a person commits suicide or when a condemned person is about to be marched into the room for the lethal shot or the throwing of the switch, Katie was calm. She was almost accepting.

Lora leaned across the table and grasped Katie's hand. "It's not going to happen, Katie. We won't let it!" The other three stopped eating and stared at her, startled by her intensity.

"I just figured out what's wrong here, your being frantic through the night and at peace this morning. You've come to the conclusion your situation's hopeless, and it's not!"

Tony looked at her through shrewdly narrowed eyes then said to Katie, "She's right, you know. Her plan's based on the fact that the road's our place of business and we drivers don't take kindly to someone threatening or hurting one of our own."

"But . . . ," Katie began.

Tony cut her off. "I've talked to some of the guys. They're not going to be obvious about it unless necessary." He leaned back against the maroon Naugahyde upholstery and reached for his coffee cup. "However, if there's any trouble, they'll be plenty evident."

Katie looked from one to the other. "But then I leave and everyone else does and then what?"

Even after it was explained again, Katie was unable to eat more than another bite or two. While Michael, who had collected all four bills and insisted upon paying them, was at the cashier's, the two women went to the restroom.

They walked out together with Lora and Michael in the front, trying to look and talk normally. She heard Tony saying in a low voice, "That's it, Katie. Head up, shoulders back, and a smile on your face no matter how hard you have to work to keep it there."

Katie murmured something and Tony began speaking of the weather as they came forward, four abreast, the men now on the outside. They were almost to Katie's panel truck when a skinny, disheveled man leaped from behind it and grabbed for her.

Tony moved quickly, thrusting himself between the two and almost knocking the shorter man off his feet. His big hand gripped Ken's shoulder, holding him at arm's length. "Hey, man, be careful when you're hurrying like that. Someone could get hurt."

His manner was as casual as though he thought the fortyish

man had accidentally bumped him. Lora decided to also give him the opportunity to save face. "Hi, Ken. Imagine seeing you here."

Ken twisted in Tony's grip, his hands clawing at his arm. "Let me go!" he shouted. Finding himself freed, he let out a string of profanity.

His wild-eyed glare took in all four of them, but focused particularly on Katie. He tried to lunge toward her but was stopped again by Tony. "I knew it, I knew you were escorting just so you could meet up with guys like these."

Katie's face was white. Her feet had not moved but Lora had the feeling she had withdrawn into herself. Her voice was trembling. "Ken, Ken, please . . . don't do this. I wasn't with either of. . . ."

He was using the foulest language Lora had ever heard. "I warned you, and you'll pay." He tried to pry Tony's strong hands from his arms but his grip had become even tighter. Ken's foot shot forward with a violent kick toward the driver's leg and he was flung like a child to the ground.

Tony stood back and watched Ken come to his feet. His slight body looked tortured and he was gasping for breath. Immediately Ken headed for Katie. "You're trash, and you travel with trash. And I'm gonna trash you!"

Katie whimpered, panic having replaced the precarious calm. She stepped backward, her small hands raised to protect her face. "Ken, please, you've got to listen. . . ."

Lora swung her bag forward, and his left knee, striking it, slowed his forward momentum and may have caused his body to turn toward her. The right-handed blow originally meant for Katie landed against her jaw.

Lora staggered backward, as much from surprise as from the blow itself. Surprisingly, she hardly felt the pain in that first moment but tasted the saltiness of her own blood. Michael caught her as she lost her balance, his face registering concern. "Are you okay?"

Suddenly the whole side of her head hurt, even her neck and ear, but she nodded. She was glad to see that Tony was behind Ken, holding him in a suffocating bear hug.

Katie sobbed, her hands reaching to touch her friend's arm. "I'm sorry, Lora, I'm so sorry!"

Michael's right arm was still around Lora as he tried to check the condition of her face, but she could not remain where she was. Looking around, she saw a circle of men and three women surrounding them.

"Trouble, Tony?" drawled a tall, angular Texan she remembered having seen Tony talking to the evening before.

Tony nodded grimly. "You might say that."

Ken was still struggling to free himself. Katie's efforts to explain she had not been misbehaving were covered by his steady stream of filth and threats.

Ken's arms were still pinned to his side but his heel kicked back hard against Tony's shin. "That's it, Ken," the driver said. Circling both of his captive's legs with his right one, Tony leaned over and threw him onto the ground.

Lora could hardly believe what she saw before her. Ken was stretched out on his stomach on the ground and Tony was sitting on his hips, holding both wrists with one hand. "This cocky little runt here has a problem," Tony said to those around them. "It seems he's been beating up his exwife, even doing it the night before she left on this run. And he's followed her through several states now, what is it, Katie? Five of them?"

"She's not my exwife!" Ken declared. "We're still married!"

Tony went on as though there'd been no interruption. "He's struck her many times, as it turns out. Worse, he's threatened her with more kinds of violence. . . ."

"Katie! Tell them, tell them you're my wife," he bawled.

Lora almost smiled at the incongruity of his commanding Katie to do anything when he was in this position. But then there was Katie's small voice. "I guess maybe, well, yes, we are still married. Legally. But we are also legally separated."

"I told you!" Ken glared at the group and now tried out a command on Tony. "You get off me, you ape!"

Tony shifted to a more comfortable position. "Be quiet, Ken," he said. "You're not in charge here, you know." As Ken resumed his tirade, Tony leaned closer. "I will make an offer, but it's the only one you get. I will stand up if you will continue to remain in exactly the position you are now until I say otherwise. And you will remain quiet. Do you understand?"

As Tony got to his feet he was followed immediately by Ken, whose fists began flailing. Just as Ken was about to land a punch in Katie's stomach, the Texan lowered a karate chop to his arm. There was a yowl of pain, followed by cries that his arm was broken and then another string of curses.

Tony moved closer, crouching slightly, his arms flexed in front like a wrestler ready to make his move. "Ken, shut your filthy mouth and behave yourself or you're going to find yourself on your back with my foot on your stomach and a gag in your mouth. Do you understand?"

Ken glared at his adversary, his anger white-hot, yet knowing Tony would do exactly as promised. Tony glanced around at the faces of those who, milling around and talking to one another, continued to give moral support. "Lora, my escort here, has some business to attend to right now and we'd sure appreciate all of you stayin' and hearin' her out."

Lora felt almost tongue-tied with embarrassment. To stand in front of these colleagues was bad enough, but now after Ken's episode and her bruised face. . . . But this had been her idea and she'd do her best to make it work.

"My name is Lora Donnavan and I've known Katie and Ken for a number of years," she began. She told of Ken's ongoing history of striking his wife and of her own part in trying to get Ken to go for counseling and in helping Katie attempt to get away from him. She spoke of the injunction against him and of his continued threats against Katie of physical torture and even death.

Lora pulled out the stack of photocopies made that morning and Michael handed two pages to each person. "As you can see, these represent an incomplete list of some of the atrocities this man has committed against Katie—everything from knocking her down, kicking her, punching her in the abdomen and causing her to miscarry—that you can look over at your leisure."

She glanced over at Katie, standing with her head down, humiliated and shamed by her marriage. She knew she'd have to involve her. "Katie, tell them what you're afraid of."

Katie's eyes looked up at her fleetingly, filled with reproach, and Tony grabbed the back of Ken's shirt and yanked him backward as he started toward her. "It's her turn now, Ken. You've got in your licks in private; let her do hers publicly."

Katie drew in a deep breath and ran the tip of her tongue across dry lips. "I'm scared to death of him and. . . ."

Lora saw the look of triumph that flickered across Ken's face and realized that, even though he was at this moment being held back by the much larger man, what he really wanted was power over Katie. Her fear had given him that.

She pushed up the sleeve of her friend's shirt. "See these bruises and the ones on her face? She has them over much of her body from what he did to her. He is totally irrational."

"I am not!" he shouted. "How'd you feel if your wife was running around all over the country, hanging out with who knows who?"

A stocky young black-haired man stepped out from what by now had become two lines of observers. "Let me tell you that Katie was my escort three or four months ago. We were on the road for thirteen days at that time, right, Katie?"

She nodded, gratitude evident on her face as he continued. "And there wasn't a time, not one single time, when I saw or heard or even suspected she was interested in making a conquest."

"One trip doesn't prove a thing," Ken declared. "Look at this trip, with two guys. . . ."

Lora interrupted his spiteful discourse. "You're way off base, Ken. I'm the escort with these two men, not Katie." She swallowed hard, almost giving in to the compulsion to explain about Michael's presence as her boss. But that would be extraneous. What was vitally important was that Katie be exonerated. "She's doing her job and to the best of my knowledge she is conscientious and does it well. . . ."

A short, bandylegged man spoke up. "She's serving as my escort now and I'll go along with what Joe, there, already said. I have nothing but respect for her and for her work and let me add that I won't take kindly to her being harassed by this jerk while she's with me."

Lora could see that people were reading some of what she'd written. "The reason I wanted all of you to get these sheets was so you would understand and so you can be witnesses. I have also," she stated, looking at Ken, "faxed copies to people back home, people who need to know."

Ken was enraged. "How dare you? I'll sue, I swear I'll get one of those lawyers who advertise on TV and sue you for everything you've got!"

She raised her brows and asked, "You'll sue me for telling the truth? Ken, there's not a lawyer with a spark of integrity who would touch your case."

"Who did you send them to?" he demanded, apparently beginning to worry as he considered possible consequences.

Lora did not answer his question.

Michael tried to get Lora to go back inside so that she might get help for her face, but she refused. They waited until Ken had entered the building and Katie and her driver took off before they left. She wouldn't discuss what she was thinking then but about noon she seemed ready to talk. "You know, Michael, I'm almost glad it happened."

"You're glad you got socked in the face?"

She must have caught the note of disbelief in his voice for she glanced at him with a crooked smile. "No, I'm not a masochist, I don't enjoy pain. But," she turned back to give attention to the highway, "I've tried many times to put myself in Katie's shoes, to try to figure out why she put up with her situation. It never made sense for her to stay there, knowing he'd undoubtedly be back doing the same, or worse."

He almost pushed her to continue, for the silence went on a long time. Finally she said, "To the best of my memory, I was never hit in the face before. Sports or accidents don't count. But to be struck deliberately, to have all of someone's hatred and strength directed toward doing harm not only physically but emotionally. . . ."

"We don't know it was emotional," he suggested.

"No, not really," she admitted. "And I'm not positive he was aiming at me at the moment of contact, though I suspect he could have pulled his punch a little if he'd so chosen. The thing is, if he just wanted to hurt me, his blow could have fallen anywhere; if he wanted to dominate me, to humiliate me to the point where I might not fight back, then aiming for my face was his best bet."

Michael studied her. From here on the right, her face looked normal. Well, maybe the upper lip was a bit puffy, but not enough to notice if you weren't looking for something. He saw her left hand move upward to cup itself around her jaw. "Does it hurt a lot?"

"Quite a bit, though it's undoubtedly mild compared with what Katie's endured."

He wished she would think more of herself and not so much about her friend. "Pain's relative, you mean?"

She laughed and her hand returned to the steering wheel. "When you come right down to it, I guess most things are." She reached for the small handbag beside her on the seat and felt around in it.

"Something I can find for you?" he offered.

Shaking her head, she retrieved a small, screw-top medicine bottle that she handed to him. "I always keep a few aspirin, antihistamines, and muscle relaxants with me when driving. Would you please get two aspirin for me and open a soda? I thought this headache would go away, but apparently it needs an assist."

The next day they were within two hours of Kansas City and making good time when the CB squawked and Tony, his voice tight, said, "Lora, I was . . . trying . . . for the next truck stop but. . . ."

"What's wrong, Tony? Are you sick?"

He sounded apologetic. "I'm . . . not sure . . . can handle it."

She put on her crisply professional manner. "Tony, tell me exactly how you feel." She heard only rasping. "Are you having chest pain? Difficulty breathing?" She shot upward a sudden prayer. *Oh, please, God, not that. . . .*

"May be . . . heart. Sorry. . . ."

Her voice must not betray her concern. She'd like to know when it started, how severe it was, and why he hadn't told her of it earlier, but nothing was as important as getting him off the highway before he lost control. "Tony, pull over and park right now."

"Can't. No . . . room on . . . shoulder." His words came out jerkily. It must take all his strength to speak at all.

"You've got to, Tony. There are children and men and women in all these cars on the highway. Get off the road for their sakes." Even if he couldn't put out the effort to save himself, she figured, he'd try for the sake of others. "I'll use my flares and reflectors to warn drivers once you're safely parked," she assured him. "Now move off, nice and slow."

He made a rumbling cough and Lora whispered to Michael, "It doesn't sound good."

The mammoth cab and trailer slowed and Lora instructed, "Put on your turn signals, Tony. And steer toward your right." She was relieved to find he could still respond and whispered, "Michael, the warning triangles and everything are in the wall rack just inside the rear, on the right."

"I've seen them. They'll be in position almost as soon as I get your keys from the ignition."

Tony's truck seemed to wobble a little but Lora's voice remained calmly supportive. "You're doing great, Tony.

Nice and steady, there . . . that's good." Her hand came out to take Michael's and she held it tight. "If you pray at all, Michael, do it now," she whispered.

"I have been," he said. "For both of you."

Although the trailer looked to be nearly stopped, it jerked violently before halting inches from the guide rail. The gold truck parked as close to it as possible. Lora checked her left rearview mirror to make sure she wouldn't be struck, opened her door, and jumped out, already running.

Through the cab window she saw Tony slumped over the steering wheel and was grateful she could open the door without fear of his falling out. She thought he might be unconscious but his thickened voice gasped, "Truck stop, twenty. . . ."

"Twenty miles away?" she guessed.

Unable to speak, Tony nodded just a little. It took all Lora's strength to straighten his body against the seat back and place his head against the rest. His shirt was soaked and large droplets of sweat were merging and running down his face.

"Oh, Tony, you did it! You got the truck off the road," she said, still encouraging him.

Her experienced fingertips felt his irregular pulse and she was desperately wishing she'd brought her medical kit when Michael appeared with it. "This help?"

"Oh, yes! Hand me the stethoscope."

She listened to his heart and lungs, checked his blood pressure, and then reached for the CB, using the emergency channel, number 9, to report the situation to the police. In a way she wished she and Michael could get him into the bed where he usually slept, but Tony was by now unresponsive.

Thank God his heart was still beating! Together they laid him across the front seat, his head pillowed on her lap, knees bent.

It was going to be difficult driving like this, but she had no choice. She needed to get him to the truck stop by the time the helicopter-ambulance arrived and she also wanted to keep checking to make sure his heart and lungs were still functioning.

"Are you sure you can manage?" Michael asked before returning to her truck to serve as her escort.

"I can," she assured him. "I do have some training with this, you know." She bent and briefly touched her cheek to his hand lying on the window frame. As she straightened, she saw puzzlement as well as worry on his face. "I'll make more calls as soon as we're on the way, so keep your line open. I'll be giving everyone this information."

She returned to channel 9 to say she was again on the road and tell of Tony's condition as best she knew it. After asking if anyone knew how to get in touch with Tony's company, less than three minutes later someone from his headquarters was on the line. In a brief and efficient manner she gave her name and Tony's, and recounted what was almost certainly a heart attack. She then gave her credentials for taking over as emergency driver of his vehicle.

Lora had known the latter information would be checked, so she wasn't surprised when she soon got the call giving her permission to keep driving. Other calls soon followed. A trucker out of Atlanta reported he was within five minutes of the truck stop and by the time they got there he'd have made sure there was sufficient space for them and the helicopter. A driver returning to Kansas City was a mile or so in front of them but would slow for her to catch up and then would lead the way. A Seattle man not far behind stated that he would "ride her tail to make sure nobody did nothing stupid" and, hearing this, one from Denver stated he was speeding up and would travel side by side with Seattle to keep people from passing or interfering in any way.

Lora felt again for Tony's pulse, thankful she had not had to stop and do CPR here on the highway. Even if that should still be needed, she knew these drivers surrounding her so protectively would give help.

She tried to discipline herself to think of nothing other than Tony's condition and controlling this huge truck which had so much more power than hers. She counted off the mileage markers beside the road. They seemed to be measuring much longer bites than indicated, even though the entourage was going the allowed 65 mph here in Missouri as compared with the 55 which would have been permitted in Pennsylvania.

While Lora's thundering heartbeats kept pace with the mighty roar of the engine, she prayed, *Oh, God, please help Tony to hold on, just for a few more miles.*

five

Lora noted more irregularities in Tony's pulse and she prayed again for wisdom. Suddenly she remembered that even though he was unconscious she might be able to reach him with her voice. This had happened too often in intensive care for her to doubt the possibility.

"Tony," she spoke clearly and distinctly, trying to ignore what anyone listening might think, "everything is under control here. We'll be meeting the ambulance in a few minutes and it will carry you safely to the hospital. In the meantime, I want your heart to beat steadily and strongly. Do you understand? Keep it steady and strong."

She did not wait for proof this was going to work before saying approvingly, "That's fine, Tony. Keep your heart steady and strong. . . ."

Dear God, thank You, she breathed silently as the atypical rhythms began to smooth out. *Please keep him safe.* "Tony, we're all praying for you and doing what we can to help. You and I are being led and are surrounded by your co-drivers, and we all really care about you. And we're counting on you to do your part."

She wondered if the excitement and turmoil that would soon be taking place might upset him. Intravenous tubes would be started as well as oxygen, and he would be placed onto a gurney or stretcher and put into the medical helicopter. Later he would be given shots, have blood taken, and receive many commands and questions.

"There will be confusion at first when we get to the truck

stop, Tony, but don't let that disturb you. You will be in good, competent hands, I promise you that."

The CB had been remarkably quiet but now the voice she recognized as that of the Kansas City driver said very softly, "Three more miles to go, Lora. I'll begin slowing within the last minute before the turn off and move in gradually. Okay?"

"Excellent," she agreed and realized Tony must sense some of what was going on as there were several hesitancies in his heartbeats. "Don't be afraid, Tony." Her fingertips stroked across his forehead and down along the side of his face and neck. "I'm right here with you and I'll stay with you until you're safely on your way to the hospital. After Michael and I deliver your load, we'll come back to see you and give our report."

She needed both hands for the wheel but didn't want to break off any contact she had established. There had been nights in pediatric intensive care when she was too busy to do anything but sing to her patients and she found herself doing that now.

"Jesus loves you, this we know, For the Bible tells us so; You and I to Him belong; We are weak but He is strong. Yes, Jesus loves you, yes, Jesus loves you, yes, Jesus loves you, the Bible tells us so.

"He really does, Tony," she assured him before continuing. "Jesus loves you, He will stay close beside you all the way. Tony, He wants me to say He is with you here today. . . ."

She was repeating the second chorus when they turned into the large paved area where a huge white helicopter was in the process of setting down in the middle of a widespread circle of men, women, and children who had gathered.

A short man in faded jeans and orange T-shirt displaying

Johnny Cash's face used wide arm motions to indicate the lead truck should drive past and Lora's cab stop near the ambulance. Two women and a man jumped out. Carrying equipment Lora recognized, they ducked under the slowing rotor blades and ran toward her.

Michael yanked open the passenger door. His gaze met hers, dropped to the face of the comatose man, and returned to Lora. "How's he doing?"

"Holding his own as far as I can tell." At that moment the doctor and paramedics were there to take over. One of them lifted the Tony's head to let her crawl out and she was surprised at needing Michael's support when her right leg buckled.

Michael's pride was written across his beaming face and echoed in his cracking voice. "Lora, you're really something! You keep coming up with surprises. . . ."

She drew back and looked at him, her head cocked. "Because my foot went to sleep?" she asked, testing gingerly then limping a few steps and rubbing her leg to help the circulation.

He laughed. "For everything else, especially for driving that monstrous truck and getting Tony here safely."

Several drivers came to congratulate Lora and to introduce themselves but Michael did most of the talking as she was busy with the medical personnel, telling what she knew concerning Tony's pain and unconscious state.

A police car arrived and the officers were with Lora as she checked through his wallet and made a record of his cash and credit cards. She also wrote down his home address and phone number and said she would call his wife right away and again with an update as soon as she and Michael got to the hospital.

Michael watched with admiration as she handled details and helped transport the stricken man to the aircraft. Just before they put him inside she said, "Dr. Bennicker, I'd like to tell him something."

"You know he can't hear you." His voice was impatient.

She showed no annoyance, but she was not to be dissuaded. "I have to try. I seemed to be making contact there in the truck."

He shrugged. "It won't hurt anything, I guess, if you don't take much time."

She leaned over the comatose man who, to Michael, looked dead except for the slightest movement in his chest. His eyes were closed and tubes already supplied oxygen through his nostrils and clear liquids through his veins. His skin was ashen even though he'd appeared to have normal coloring when they'd eaten together that morning.

Michael was close enough to see her hand stroking the patient's arm. "Tony, this is Lora. You're going to be fine, take my word for that. Just keep your heart pumping nice and regular and the trip to the hospital will be smooth and your time there okay. Remember, Tony, we're continuing to pray and you keep yourself calm and your heartbeat regular." She kissed him on the cheek and backed away.

She stood straight and smiled at the young physician. "Thank you, doctor. Positive input helped many of my patients when I was an intensive care supervisor. I'd feel derelict in my duty if I hadn't given it to this man I respect and like."

Obviously not impressed, he didn't answer or so much as look at or speak to her. One of the paramedics, however, glanced from the doctor to her and winked.

With an almost deafening roar the rotor blades started

turning. Dust and dirt flew through the air and Michael clasped Lora's hand to lead her away from the shiny whirlwind. It seemed to hover in the sky for a moment before heading south toward Kansas City, the racket gradually lowering in volume and pitch.

Lora was more relaxed now that Tony was cared for. People wanted information about him and she gave it easily but she also stressed the need for their continued praying. She thanked those who had gone out of their way to help and even shared sodas and chips with the drivers around a shaded picnic table.

Ted, of Seattle, told her as they headed back to their vehicles, "You blew my mind when you started singing. I didn't know whether he was awake or had died or what."

Atlanta smiled. "And I believe you sorta changed those words too."

"I did," she admitted. "I try to make it as personal as possible. 'If I love Him 'till I die, He will take me home on high' and other stanzas in different versions speak of death. I wanted to stress life right then, getting well."

They already knew of her hospital experience and Michael suspected there'd be speculation by many when they later considered the incongruity of her employment as an escort.

Dwayne, the stocky trucker returning to Kansas City, found their destination to be within two miles of where he was heading. Although a police car led them the rest of the way, Dwayne followed along and even took them as his guests to a Chinese restaurant he liked.

Michael and Lora went to the hospital immediately afterward. At first there was some doubt they'd be allowed to see Tony since they weren't members of his family, but Lora's hospital experience again came in handy.

"Hello there, you remarkable man," Lora greeted the patient as they entered.

Tony weakly reached a hand to each of them as they came up alongside his hospital bed, the head of which was sharply elevated. Bottles of clear and yellowish liquids were hanging from metal poles and oxygen was entering both nostrils through plastic tubing. His attempted smile was almost a grimace because of the pain. "I understand you two saved my life."

She squeezed his hand, careful not to disturb the IV just above the wrist. "No, Tony, God did. But He let us help."

Michael sighed. "I think you may have shortened mine! You gave me quite a scare."

"I've been lying here considering how stupid I am," Tony confessed. "I thought it was just heartburn these past two weeks."

"Never thought of going to a doctor, did you?" she asked.

"Well," his heavy lids drooped over sunken eyes, "I do have an appointment for next week but . . . I think I won't make that."

They couldn't visit long, and wouldn't have even had Tony not explained he hurt all over. " . . . Like my Peterbilt ran over me."

"Just one more thing," Lora said. "When we talked with your wife the second time she said her flight arrives at eight-seventeen this evening. We're meeting her at the airport and bringing her right here, but we won't come in."

There were tears in Tony's eyes. "I appreciate your picking her up. Phyl never—went ahead with things—never traveled alone. Finding a bus, getting a taxi, would be scary for her."

"We're looking forward to getting to know her," Lora said.

"She seems like a fine woman."

"The finest." He yawned then apologized, but they assured him they were leaving and he should try to sleep.

It felt right to Michael to have Lora's hand resting on his arm. He matched his stride to hers as they went to the parking lot and was surprised and pleased when she handed him her keys. "You've been here before, so you can chauffeur while I look around."

"It's a beautiful city, well worth admiring," he told her. "I've been told how many fountains and monuments they have, but don't remember. I believe it's more than any other city west of the Mississippi. In fact, it's known as 'The City of Fountains.'" After his semiguided tour she had no doubts he could find gainful employment in the travel industry should he tire of his business.

"What would you like to do tomorrow?" he asked while driving out to the airport.

"I usually do my homework ahead of time when I've got a weekend layover," she said. "I spend hours with my AAA maps and write-ups and ask people what I should see. But this time I didn't. You know, Dwayne mentioned some interesting side trips. Kansas City was where the wagon trains got outfitted before they left for the West. I suppose that museum would be interesting, and, oh yes, the Truman home in Independence, a suburb of Kansas City."

"And the Royals have a home game tomorrow."

She laughed. "From your conversations with Tony, I assume that should have scheduling priority."

He remembered her not having participated in their conversations of RBIs, free agents, farm teams, and the like. "You'd rather not?"

Her head tilted slightly. "It's not something I'd do if I were here alone, but I'm sure it will be fun with you." And then she explained, "I'll have to admit I've never been to a game or watched one on TV, for that matter."

His hand reached to cover hers on the seat. "Don't feel you have to. . . ."

"I don't. I was just warning you that I'll probably have dozens of dumb questions or may even cheer for the wrong team."

The fifteen miles to the airport passed quickly and at this hour they found a parking spot near the terminal. They were a little early so, after finding that Phyl's plane was to arrive on time, they wandered through several shops.

He heard an exclamation of dismay as she stopped before a rack of attractive greeting cards. "Oh dear, this is Sally's birthday and I never sent a card or called!"

She pulled out one after another, reading then replacing them. "It's hard to find the right message for my sister," she said. "Depending on her state of mind, she could take offense at something as innocuous as 'Have a good day.' "

"Well, might she go for one of these humorous ones?" he suggested.

She joined him in reading them, but all were rejected as too mushy, flip, or otherwise unsuitable. While going through a section specifically for sisters, she decided on one. He was grateful she didn't ask for his input. He didn't know Sally and wasn't sure he wanted to. No, on second thought, he *did* want to meet Sally and her mother and anyone—everyone— important in Lora's life.

Tony's wife had described herself as only five feet tall, with short, light brown hair sort of puffed out over the ears, and wearing a white linen jacket and a flowered skirt. Happily, for Lora and Michael, that was more than adequate.

She had not mentioned, however, how worried she'd be looking, but they expected that.

Michael took her carry-on bag and as they waited at the carousel for her suitcase and then started for the car they filled her in on what had happened. "I kept telling him he should have a checkup, but he wouldn't," Phyl said.

"Perhaps this wasn't as much of a shock to him as we'd thought," Michael suggested. "At least he'd made that doctor's appointment for next week."

"He had?" She rubbed her hand across her forehead. "He didn't tell me. . . ."

Lora stood back for Phyl to precede her through the terminal door. "I suspect he wanted to keep you from worrying. As you know, health problems like this are bad for long-distance drivers. I'm sure he wouldn't want to say or do anything until he was sure."

Phyl stopped right in the middle of the street. "Will he have to quit?"

Michael's hands were full so it was Lora who took her arm and started her forward again. "It's probably too soon to tell. Thank God it was less than an hour from when his pain got really bad to when the doctor gave the special clot-busting medicine. We hope his heart may not have much or any permanent damage."

"You think he'll be able to return to trucking?" she persisted.

"You'll know before we do. You should have an opportunity to talk with the cardiologist tomorrow morning."

"But that's Saturday. Maybe he won't be in. . . ."

"Well, either he or another specialist representing him will be checking Tony. We'll ask the nurses tonight when he usually comes and tell them you definitely need to speak with him or her in the morning."

Lora must have seen the uncertainty for she squeezed Phyl's arm. "Don't be afraid to be firm, not nasty, of course, but firm. Tony's your husband and they must keep you informed of what's happening. Some don't do a good job at it unless you push them."

Michael wasn't sure she was convinced. "Phyl, Lora is a nurse and worked for years in an intensive care unit. She's dealt with families and with doctors and knows what she's talking about."

Phyl visibly relaxed. "Then that's what I'll do," she announced and, that decision made, they were able to talk of her trip and the arrangements made for the two teens still at home.

Michael left the women at the hospital's front door and Lora went with Phyl to the cardiac care unit. Expecting her back soon, he parked illegally in the physicians' lot, since there were a number of empty spaces.

He had not checked his watch when returning to the hospital, but it seemed like a long time before Lora's return.

"What a day!" she exclaimed, sinking down into the seat.

The truck started smoothly and he realized she must take good care of it.

"I'm sure you're exhausted," he sympathized.

"I am, though I didn't realize it till now. I was so involved keeping Phyl calm I didn't have time for much else."

"Did you go in with her?"

"Um-hmm. I hadn't expected to, in fact, had told her I wouldn't. But she seemed so upset I felt I had to stay a while."

"How is she now?"

"Okay, I think. One of the residents came to check Tony

while we were there and he assured her, as had the nurses, that Tony is, quote, 'doing as well as can be expected.' "

"I take it that means many things."

"Yes, but actually that is about all anyone can say at this point. The monitors show his pulse, respiration, and EKG readings are good and apparently his initial blood work came through fine. I told her what they mean and there's no reason in the world for her staying there all night."

Michael looked at her sharply. "She's not planning to?"

Lora pushed the hair back from her forehead. "She expected to, but I talked her out of it and checked on motel and bed-and-breakfast accommodations. I phoned a couple of them and called a taxi to come for her in an hour." She yawned, apologized, then said, "I offered to take her now, but she wanted to stay for the next visiting time."

He looked at her and smiled. "We all need a good night's sleep, Lora."

She agreed. "I think you're right."

There'd been other times she'd been this tired, but this was the first she'd let herself get so exhausted on the road. She must get her card sent to Sally. She'd thought she would call tonight, but with the time change it would be nearly half-past eleven back home. She'd do it in the morning.

She awakened several times during the night and found herself worrying about Katie. And about her mother. She'd never thought of it this way before but right now she considered them both victims. Each was loving and selfless, and each had been taken advantage of. At least Katie had finally gone through with signing a warrant against Ken. Would Mom ever be free?

And what of herself? Was she almost as weak? She had tried pushing Sally into physical and occupational therapy, and been considered hard and feelingless because of that. She had also insisted that Mom appeal to various agencies for help, with the purpose of finding someone to assist with Sally's care or even to stay with her while her mother left the house for a few hours. Lora finally went ahead with this on her own, and her family still blamed her for Sally's "relapse" that time.

Between runs she continued to try to spare Mom who got the chance then to go to the store to replace canned and frozen foods, paper products, and other items used during the previous week or two.

She also went to church or to visit elderly relatives in nursing homes and to accompany a woman friend to a movie or for dinner. Lora sorely missed going to her church and Sunday school. Would it be too much for Mom and her to take turns?

I've got so much advice for other people, she mocked herself. *Why can't I help Lora Donnavan for a change?* She turned and tossed and finally went back to sleep. By the time she awakened she had to hurry to shower and get dressed for her morning with Michael. She didn't realize she was humming until she put words to her tune. "My morning with Michael," she sang, then stopped immediately, staring at herself in the mirror.

Mornings with Michael. That had a nice sound. A very nice sound. She smiled at her reflection and went to answer his knock at the door.

six

When Lora opened the door, Michael couldn't hold back the first words that came to his mind. "Wow!" he exclaimed. "What a knockout I've been riding with this week!"

He clasped her upper arms as gently and carefully as he would hold a priceless painting. His gaze slowly moved from her beautiful eyes down over the daintily embroidered cotton knit blouse, softly flowing silk skirt, and white sandals encasing small, slender feet.

Her magnificent blue eyes held him in their gaze. "I knew you were lovely from that first moment I saw you, Lora, but you're far more than that." A flush crept up onto her face and he leaned over to kiss her cheek.

It was a light kiss, one that could be safely given to an elderly aunt or a two year old, and yet she drew in her breath quickly and turned as though to move away from him. "Did you . . . sleep well, Michael?"

Under the circumstances it wasn't appropriate to tell her he'd been thinking about her far too much. He reluctantly released her. "Quite well, thanks. And you?"

She laughed. "I almost overslept, actually. But I'm ready now."

Ah, yes, she certainly was, he thought. She hadn't responded favorably to his earlier compliment and he didn't want her defenses to go up any further. "Shall we eat here at the motel or wander around till we see something we like?"

Her reaction was almost childlike as her face lit up and her hands came together. "Let's wander."

They walked to a small nearby park with a centrally located fountain and manicured grass and plantings. Sitting on the coping facing one another, they trailed their fingers in the water and spoke of their childhood or, rather, he did and she kept asking questions.

He considered his early years typical or ordinary. However, he couldn't miss her wistfulness as he told of his parents taking him and his sister camping and fishing, of the family playing games around the kitchen table on rainy evenings, and their going to the zoo together. Even having all the kids on the block in their backyard for games and fun seemed to enthrall her.

"I hope," she said as they left the fountain to walk down the sidewalk, "you appreciate what you have."

"What?"

She looked straight ahead and he wished he could see her eyes. "You have such beautiful memories, Michael. They must serve as a reservoir of strength when things go wrong."

"I never thought of them that way, but you're right, of course." The pebble he kicked skittered in front of them. "I don't remember ever doubting my folks's love for me, though when I needed discipline I did question how they could do that to someone they cared about."

Her pensive state seemed to vanish when they entered what had appeared to be a small eatery but turned out to be larger than expected. The bright and cheerful rooms seemed the perfect antidote for her troubled thoughts. "I'm sure that question got answered when you had children of your own."

"You can, indeed, be sure of that." There was an empty booth by the second window and he steered Lora in that direction. "My task may be even more difficult than my parents' in that my children don't have a mother. It's essential they not feel deprived of love."

"Yes," she agreed. "That has to be your priority."

He tried again to get her to speak of her childhood but the waitress arrived then and when he pitched a question afterward she changed the subject. She commented that the sausages and pancakes she had ordered weren't quite as good as the spicy country ones of southern Pennsylvania.

He enjoyed watching her as she ate, noting how her eyes lit up when she laughed at something he said. She teased him about having parked the night before in the doctors' area as she carefully filled his empty tea cup from her very large glass of orange juice.

They returned to the motel, picked up her truck, and headed for the hospital, a trip that seemed shorter this morning with the bright clear sky overhead and variegated flowers in bloom. Two swallows swooped over the parking area and they wondered out loud where they would nest in Kansas City.

Lora wasn't surprised to find Phyl curled up in a comfortable chair in cardiac care's visitor's lounge. "You did go to the motel last night, didn't you?"

The petite woman set the somewhat-rumpled *Reader's Digest* back on a stand with an uneven stack of other magazines. "Oh, yes. I went down at the right time and the taxi came on schedule and delivered me to the door of the motel. No trouble at all. Thanks to you."

Lora's hand flipped outward in a dismissive gesture. "Did you get any rest?"

Phyl's expression showed some guilt as well as surprise. "I did, though I hadn't expected to."

Lora smiled as she sat in the chair to her right while Michael sank into the opposite one. "You were exhausted, and not only physically. How's your husband doing this morning?"

"The nurses say he's getting along well. I've been in twice so far and, though I don't know what to look for like you do, he seems good." She hesitated before stating her concerns, "He's still having lots of pain, though he doesn't want to talk about it. And he didn't sleep much."

Lora explained, "Nobody does the first night. The staff's constantly doing something, taking blood, giving shots, what have you. . . ."

"He did mention that, but he wasn't complaining!" Phyl added quickly, probably considering this was what Lora would have been doing were she employed in this unit.

It wasn't long before a nurse came to say one or two visitors could come in. Phyl insisted Lora and Michael go, since she'd be here all day. Michael offered to wait while the women entered, but Phyl wouldn't hear of it.

Lora touched the nurse's arm as they went through the double doors. "Has his cardiologist been in this morning?"

"Not yet. Well, he was here for an emergency during early morning hours and checked your patient then, but he should be coming back any minute now."

"Good. His wife flew in last night from Pennsylvania and she needs to talk with him."

The young woman nodded. "I know. It's in the notes."

They saw Tony before he knew they were there. His eyes were closed and his large hands lay loosely upon the sheet. He wasn't asleep, not with that tight, set look on his face, but with all the other sounds he didn't recognize the difference their steps made.

When they were beside his bed Lora's hand slipped into his before he opened his eyes. For a split second he looked puzzled before a wide smile spread across his face. His grip was almost painful. "Lora, Michael! It's good of you to come."

"No, it's not good of us, we couldn't not come," she assured him.

Michael, clasping the other hand, emphasized this. "You had us plenty worried yesterday, Tony. We had to see how much better you are this morning."

Tony told of his night and that he still had pain throughout his body and not just in his chest. Lora figured this must have been explained before, but she went over again that the decreased circulation caused by the heart attack was making his body cells cry out for more oxygen.

"That's going to be better soon," she promised and then, while they visited for their allotted time, her skilled fingers massaged his left shoulder, arm, and neck. She could feel as well as see him relaxing as she also assured him his monitor's EKG tracings and the continuing flashing of pulse rate and blood pressure indicated his body was doing a good job.

There was a long wait to get into the National Frontier Trails Center at Independence, the "Queen City of Trails." Disappointed, Michael had looked forward to learning more of the Oregon, California, and Santa Fe trails, all of which had started in Independence. One could also visit the spring from which the brave, adventurous, or desperate men, women, and children had filled their water barrels. Lora also would have been interested in the historical film and artifacts and diaries of the pioneers who had followed their dreams by moving west.

Michael drove through Independence and found the Harry S. Truman Historical District. Neither of them knew a great

deal about him other than that he'd become president following the death of Franklin Delano Roosevelt and had a
difficult time convincing people he was the right man for the
job.

They bought tickets for a tour of the Truman home but
stayed at the tourist center long enough to see the movie
about his life, and for Michael to buy Lora several of the
mystery books by Margaret Truman. Delighted that Michael
remembered her late-night avocation, Lora accepted them
with pleasure.

They were charmed by the Trumans' three-storied white
Victorian house with its inviting gingerbread-trimmed veranda set back a distance from the locked wrought iron gate
and fence. The casual plantings and surroundings made it
look homey, a trait that carried over to the interior as well.
The kitchen had not been upgraded even when the president
and Mrs. Truman returned after living in the White House,
but the large dining room was much more formal and the
table setting lovely.

Michael noted Lora's fascination with the account
given by the National Parks Service guide concerning life
here, especially the part about President Truman's
mother-in-law. While she lived with them she was constantly making the point that the president "wasn't good
enough for her daughter."

They stood with other tourists in the high-ceilinged, large,
light hallway separating the two front rooms. The president's
walking stick and coat hung beside the more secluded rear
exit, a reminder of the days when he would sneak away from
his Secret Service protectors so he could take his rapid
morning walks.

Lora was quiet after leaving. Following their map, they

found the courthouse where Mr. Truman had served for many years before going to Washington. Suddenly she said, "Isn't it amazing? Lawyer, judge, congressman, vice-president, and president, yet his mother-in-law could never see how great he was."

"Thank God he didn't need that commendation, though I'm sure he'd have welcomed it." He placed his hand under her elbow as they went down the steps on the way back to the truck. "He and his wife and daughter—and the world—knew what he was capable of and the importance of what he accomplished. Sadly, the mother-in-law will probably be remembered only for her bitterness and lack of love."

Lora sighed, and he heard her repeat slowly, "Bitterness and lack of love. . . ."

How Michael wished the young woman beside him would share the stresses that must be making life difficult for her. This foray into the Truman hometown had obviously unearthed some painful memories.

They decided they still had time to go back into the city to the exhibits in the Hallmark Visitors Center, housed in Hall's Crown Center Complex, before going to the Royals game.

Michael took pleasure in Lora's enjoyment of the historical displays of greeting cards and the demonstration of techniques used in making them through the years. While she watched a press operator demonstrate processes used in producing a greeting card, it boggled her mind that they could possibly sell the over 11 million of them made each day.

As they returned to the truck she murmured, "I don't think I'll ever again just go in a store for a card, ribbon, or wrapping paper without some appreciation of what goes into making them."

"That's true of most things—and people—isn't it?"

Michael observed. "Once we get past first impressions, we find so much more there than we dreamed."

She looked at him from the corner of her eyes. "Like the president?"

"And you. And even me."

The smile slowly left her face as she turned fully toward him. Her eyes, though still warm, became enigmatic. "Even you, Michael. And me."

She got into the truck and gently placed on the dashboard her silvery ribbon star bow, a souvenir of her day with Michael.

Lora apologized for having to park such a distance from the Harry S. Truman Sports Complex. "I didn't realize how long I was spending with the cards."

"We're fine," he assured her. "I already have our tickets. With the binoculars and hoagies in your bag, we'll see and eat to our hearts' content."

As far as she could remember Lora had never even seen pictures of the fantastic side-by-side stadiums, the only such complex in the nation. The first, he informed her as they hurried by, was called the Arrowhead and was the home of football's Kansas City Chiefs. The one beside it, toward which people were streaming from all directions, was named for the home baseball team, the Kansas City Royals.

She glanced at her watch as they reached the ramp leading to the third deck, on the first-base side. They hurried upward, part of an excited, pushing, enthusiastic crowd. Michael seemed to know exactly where they should be going and she followed him around the outside curve of the massive, sun-reflecting structure.

He led her through a passageway under the next higher

level and into the open again, out where there were uncounted rows of seats, most already occupied. Lora was
grateful that at least for now they were in the shade, but she
suspected from the sun's position and the time of day that this
would soon change.

As Michael pointed out the twelve-story electronic
scoreboard and the dancing fountains, she exclaimed, "I
never dreamed they could make such a huge TV screen!"

"It's the biggest in the country. This is the first stadium to
use this particular display board."

"If we're going to watch the game on TV, wouldn't it have
been more comfortable to stay in the motel?"

He looked toward her, startled. "For a moment I thought
you meant that." He was obviously relieved at her teasing
grin. "You'll see how helpful it is when the players are
introduced and the announcer tells of their backgrounds and
specific skills. Or, when someone does something especially
well, we'll get a better look at it."

She could wait to find out about that. In the meantime, she
took the first sandwich from her bag and held it toward him.
"Ready?"

He reached for it. "You're joining me, aren't you?"

"Sure am. If the game's as good as you're anticipating, we
may be too excited later to know what we're eating."

He took a big bite and chewed it with obvious enjoyment.
"That's a better excuse for eating right now than any I could
have come up with."

They had not quite finished eating when the teams came
running onto the field. Lora became immediately grateful for
the screen. Not only did it tell who each player was and what
he looked like, what number he wore, and what position he
played, best of all, it indicated which teams they were on. She

was thus spared the humiliation of having to ask Michael. Michael did inform her that as the home team the Royals were wearing white uniforms with blue trim.

The game seemed slower than expected until she remembered that snatches shown at the end of the evening news were a compilation of the high points of games from all teams of both leagues. She smiled at how Michael would laugh if she confessed these thoughts.

She made an effort to pay attention to what was happening down on the field. However, her mind wandered everywhere from where they were sitting, now in the extreme heat of the sun. She thought of Katie driving westward, Tony in the intensive care unit across the city, and Sally in her bed back home.

What could she do about Sally? Was it possible to use tough love, to make her do some things for herself? That sounded good but Lora didn't know how to make or implement a workable plan.

Someone made a home run with one player on second base and she jumped up to cheer with Michael while both men circled the bases and were greeted with hugs and congratulatory pummeling by teammates.

Michael turned to give her a spontaneous hug, lifting her right off her feet, but then he turned back to the game. She suspected he would not even remember this unconscious manifestation of happiness at his team's good showing, but she would.

The tip of her tongue licked her dry lips that tasted salty. Perspiration was making her face wet and her clothing stick to her. She should have worn one of her soft knit T-shirts or the buttoned cotton shirts she'd packed. *If you had any common sense . . .* , she told herself.

She waited until the visiting team came to bat before nudging Michael. "I could sure use a soda right now. Can I get you one too?"

He looked startled, then jumped to his feet. "Here, you stay. I'll get them."

She had to grab his arm to stop him. "Please let me. I'd rather go, honestly I would."

He probably thought she was being kind and sank back into his seat. When she glanced back from the passageway through which they'd come earlier, Lora smiled crookedly. He was cheering along with the crowd over something about which she had only the foggiest idea.

She sipped her drink slowly, resisting the urge to gulp it down as her thirsting body demanded. She had felt no movement of air while seated, but in the shaded passageway there were faint stirrings. She stood there a while before again braving the ovenlike conditions.

Michael's thanks were almost mechanical as she handed the soda to him just as a pinch hitter lobbed a ball into the stands off to their right. The crowd erupted with shouts and cheers and the screen was filled with reruns of the scene and the man racing around the bases and little cartoon characters going crazy with excitement.

Things calmed down a bit and Lora was pleased at her newfound ability to recognize some names and remember if a particular batter had got a hit on a previous trip to the plate. Between innings she asked whether the large flags on the towering poles across from them had some special significance. Michael thought each of them represented a league championship, and the man next to him pointed to the especially tall one that celebrated the Royals' 1985 World Championship.

A number of spectators around her were getting burned and she wished she'd brought some sunscreen. *One of the many benefits of attending a game*, she thought wryly.

The seventh inning stretch finally came. Getting up, Michael and Lora went for refills on drinks, then walked around the deck's outside curve. He asked if she wanted something to eat, but she declined and he enthusiastically continued speaking of how great the game was, marvelous specific plays, and how grateful he was to be here.

She asked questions and tried to show interest, and apparently didn't make any terribly bad mistakes. He was probably so excited he didn't notice. At this point she'd settle for either!

She minded the heat even more during the later innings. She wondered why the "stretch" came so near the end of the game. Wouldn't one nearer the middle—perhaps a fifth-inning one—be better? Suppose your team was far behind at that time. Wouldn't you be more likely to hope then for your men to do better and make the game more interesting? She was sure she'd leave by the seventh inning of a lopsided game. But what did she know about it? This contest had been close enough all along that either team might win.

When the Royals at last claimed the victory, Lora and Michael left the stadium amid a general outpouring of happiness and good will. "Did you have a good time, Lora?" Michael asked as they were stopped for a time by the exiting streams of vehicles.

Her gaze remained on the traffic. "Better than I thought I would." She thought she'd have a good time anywhere with Michael.

"Great! I thought you'd like baseball once you saw a game live."

They spoke of circling around to the hospital on the way back to where they were staying but Lora hesitated. "After sitting in the sun this long, I need a shower before going anywhere."

"Me, too." He pulled the damp knit cotton away from his chest but, when released, it clung to him again. "Would you like to rest a while before going for dinner?"

She hadn't thought that far ahead. "I'm tired enough right now to do that, but my shower will probably perk me up. I want to check your arm again and change the dressing on it. With everything happening yesterday, I forgot about it until after I was in bed."

It looked as though his right hand was pressing firmly against the bandage. "I'm sure it's doing fine," he told her.

"I still want to look at it and put on a fresh bandage."

He grinned. "Always the nurse, aren't you?"

"When there's sickness or injury, yes."

He looked at her with apologetic concern and reached to gently touch her left cheek. "And how is your injury?"

"I thought for sure I'd be black and blue, since it did swell some at first." She held still for his close inspection. "It looks okay, doesn't it?"

His gentle fingers moved along her jaw then upward to her high cheekbone and finally down under her chin. "Very much okay, Lora," he assured her. "But how does it feel?"

"There's only a little sensitivity, and that's when I'm checking, you know, moving my jaw into unusual positions, that sort of thing."

He shook his head sadly. "He really clobbered you!"

"He did, didn't he? I never thought I'd get hit. If I had, I'd have been prepared to step back." Gazing into his eyes, she took her words one step further.

And I didn't expect to feel like this about you, either, Michael. If I had, perhaps I'd have been prepared to step back from that, also.

seven

Her bed looked inviting as she prepared for her shower. Once again she was glad she had been born with curly hair. A quick towel dry was all it needed and she'd look as she had hours earlier. At least that was one good thing she'd received from her father. That and her height. Mom was only about five-foot one and, Lora made an effort to remember, Sally was about that also.

Sally. Today was her birthday. Was she in as terrible a mood as last year when Lora didn't get back from a run until after ten at night?

Her shower finished, she propped herself against the bed's headboard and reached for the phone. Lora's mother answered it on the fifth ring.

"Hi, Mom, how are you?"

The voice became petulant. "Not very good. My arthritis is acting up something awful, especially in the lower back and in my neck."

"I'm sorry. Did it just start?"

Lora could have predicted the answer and she knew she shouldn't have asked. "The day you left's when it got bad. Though I told you the day before that it was starting."

She sounded accusing as usual, and Lora smothered a sigh. "We must get in touch with the agencies again about sending you help, Mom. This lifting and turning is too much for you when you feel this way."

Sally came on the phone too and Lora could picture her lying there with it propped in position so she could easily

hear and speak. "Your getting a sensible job and not gallivanting off like you do all the time would solve the problem,
Lora."

Lora did not wish to get dragged into that right now. "Hi,
Sally. I'm calling to wish you a happy birthday."

"So that's why you called. I was wondering. It's been a
week since you left and you haven't even called once."

Lora forced a laugh. "Where I am, the weeks are still seven
days long, Sally. I'd better get you a calendar."

The voice was full of self-pity. "If you had any idea of
how slow time passes when you're flat on your back all the
time. . . ."

Lora did not try to stem the flow of words, but she didn't
pay too much attention either. Except for a change of word
here and there it was the same speech given every time there
was a discussion, argument, or harangue. She watched the
second hand on her watch go around once, twice, three times.
Sally finally slowed enough to demand, "So what do you
have to say about that, Lora?"

She wasn't sure if there was a specific "that" being considered but she tried to play it safe. "Well, I hope things go better
for you both, Sally. I'm not sure when I'll be back."

"Where are you now?"

"In Missouri. Kansas City, actually."

"Did you just get there today?"

Lora hoped to defuse what she suspected would be coming
next. "Yesterday, but I've spent much of the time at the
hospital. The driver I was escorting had a heart attack shortly
before arriving here, so I brought the big truck the rest of the
way."

"Where's yours, then?"

Lora must sound totally irresponsible. "Another driver

brought mine to my destination, so I've got it now." She
cleared her throat. "I can't meet the next load until early
Monday morning, when I'll be heading for a place near
Atlanta. Perhaps I will get a northbound trip from there."

Mom asked, "Is there any point in saving you some
birthday cake?"

Lora was pleased to be asked. "I'd like that. Would you put
a piece in the freezer for me?"

"It's one you especially like, double fudge with peanut
butter frosting."

"Ummm. It sounds delicious. I'll look forward to it."

Sally said, in what Lora assumed was supposed to sound
like teasing but was undoubtedly a dig, "I presume you were
too busy to buy me a birthday card."

"Oh, I did get one, and you'll receive it soon. With
everything happening, I neglected to mail it."

She should have known better than to say that. Sally
immediately jumped on the "fact" that everything and everyone else in the world got preferential treatment from Lora.

Lora again watched the second hand rotating and thought
of the phone bill she'd have to pay. She had considered
already just hanging up when Sally got into one of these
monologues, but she knew she wouldn't. Especially on
Sally's birthday.

She had little time before Michael would be here. "Sally
. . . ," she tried to interrupt, and then, "Sally!" Before the
flow of words could get underway again, Lora said, "I have
to meet someone to go to the hospital."

"It's some man, isn't it?"

She put her own twist on that one. "The patient is a man,
from near Philadelphia. His wife flew in last night so I met
her at the airport and took her to the hospital." She felt guilty

about implying she was meeting Phyl, but she would be in a little while. "I've got to go now, Sally. I hope the rest of your birthday is what you'd like it to be."

But she could not hang up the phone for another couple of minutes. She returned it to its cradle, swung her long legs over the side of the bed, and stood up. Compared with some calls, this conversation had gone fairly well. There had been no crying or absolute insistence on her getting home right away. Lora's earnings now were not compared to what they'd be if she went back to her real job, nursing. No interest in Lora's experiences had been shown or in how she'd managed with driving the large truck, or in Tony's condition.

In fact nothing that didn't directly touch Sally's life meant much to her, except for all her soap operas. The heroines of the various daytime dramas Sally regarded as personal friends who lived glamorous and exciting, but tragic, existences.

Lora crossed to the exposed closet area to check the limited wardrobe she'd brought with her. Since she'd already worn the one skirt today, her choices lay between the long blue linen skirt with white dots or her slim black pants. She decided to save the skirt and lacy blouse for church tomorrow.

She dressed and went to the bathroom to apply lipstick and to run a comb through her still-damp hair. She didn't often use blush and definitely didn't need it now as her face was pink from the afternoon's sun.

Michael had not set an exact time of arrival, so she carried one of his gift mysteries to the chair by the window. The knock on the door came before she'd even seated herself.

His eyes were lit with admiration. "I was planning to ask you to go with me to a restaurant specializing in Kansas

City's famed barbecued ribs, but erase that. Anyone looking like you must dine at a place with white-linen tablecloths and be served that other K. C. specialty, strip steak. How does that sound?"

"Wonderful!" she agreed. On second thought she wasn't sure she meant the ribs, the steak, or the handsome man resplendent in white pants, pin-striped shirt with open collar, and navy blazer.

"Let's go to the hospital first, before we eat," she suggested and he agreed. They found Phyl looking less tired and also less worried than in the morning. Her meeting with the heart specialist had relieved some of her earlier anxiety.

Tony had made peace with the pain insofar as asking for pills was concerned, finally accepting that bearing it—toughing it out—wasn't helping his heart to get better. He visited with them more easily and his naturally optimistic outlook showed. He did, however, again ask Lora's opinion as to whether he'd be back driving and was able to smile a little when she told him he was to ask the doctor questions like that.

Phyl had eaten an early supper in the hospital cafeteria and didn't accept Lora's invitation to join them. They were nearly to the truck when Michael asked in an apologetic voice, "Would you be terribly disappointed if we put off that steak dinner till tomorrow, Lora? I'm afraid we won't have . . . you see, I was going to tell you while we were eating. I got tickets to the road company performance of 'My Fair Lady,' which is playing at the Starlight Theater."

"That sounds delightful! With a name like Starlight, is the theater outdoors?" she asked.

"In Swope Park. There's an excellent zoo there, too, I understand."

"I love zoos! Might that be a possibility for tomorrow

afternoon? After church and dinner?"

He helped her into the truck. "Sounds great." He circled to the driver's side and opened the door she'd leaned across to unlock.

Growing up in Pennsylvania, with its mountainous terrain, Lora was used to the sun setting earlier than here on the plains. To her the hour seemed much earlier but she quickly readjusted her thinking. "A fast food place would be fine with me," she suggested.

He looked at her with a wry grin. "This big spender sure knows how to impress a girl!"

She laughed. "Your intentions were good. And it was I who suggested we stop at the hospital for the few minutes that became much longer."

"We'll accept the blame jointly."

"I'd like to pay for my own meals and everything, Michael. You bought the tickets for the game and those for tonight's play. Please let me pay you back." Stating her policy always made her feel a little uncomfortable, but he had to know.

"Why?"

He had not looked at her as he asked the question and she wondered if that were because of the traffic, which did merit attention, or because he was giving her room to express herself. "Well, if I were alone on this run I'd be paying my own way."

"And would you have gone to the game this afternoon?"

"Well, no. Because I wouldn't have thought of doing that."

"And would you be going to a play tonight?"

She had to admit, "I don't like going by myself to things like that."

"I don't either." He reached to squeeze her hand as he went

logically through his reasoning. "I did want to see the game and do want to see the play, and your presence makes that possible. Therefore, the ticket costs are mine. Without them, I wouldn't have these two parts of this lovely day, memories of which I will always treasure."

She did not respond until he glanced her way again. "Sure you're not a lawyer or something?"

He laughed. "It would have to be the 'something'."

Yes, indeed, Michael, you are something, something inexplicably precious, inexplicably exciting, she thought delightedly. She pointed toward a seafood chain restaurant ahead on their right. "How does that look?"

The turn signals clicked on, the truck slowed, and they were soon stopped in the large parking lot. She feared there'd be a long waiting line, but they were seated within a few minutes.

"This is fine with me," she reassured Michael when he tried again to apologize for not taking her for the steak tonight. "We seldom ate fish or seafood at home. Once I discovered what I had been missing, during my college years I quickly made up for not having eaten my quota till then. And I must be way over that by now."

Michael wondered if he could have picked her up earlier at her room. He hadn't wanted to rush her but it would have helped the time situation. He supposed he should have guessed she'd like to go to the hospital again before eating, but he was still learning how strong her loyalties were.

She had seemed on edge when she walked down the hallway with him, and yet she'd done everything right. Perhaps he had read too much into what he considered almost a nervous laugh when he asked if she got through on her call home.

"Did Sally have a nice birthday?" he ventured while removing the shell from another shrimp.

A shadow slipped over her countenance. "As nice as Sally permits herself to have," Lora said without looking up.

"She makes your life miserable, doesn't she?"

She drew in a deep breath and her eyes met his. "I apparently owe you an apology. I'm coming across as a martyr. . . ."

"Anything but a martyr, Lora. I suspect you find yourself in a bind you're not sure how to get out of." She gave the slightest of nods but said nothing and he offered, "Want to talk about it?"

He was relieved that she at least hesitated before shaking her head. "No. Not now, anyway."

"Would you let me help? You know I . . . like and admire you. If there's anything I can do, I'd welcome that opportunity."

The brightness in her eyes were unshed tears. "Thank you, Michael. I appreciate that but this is to be our night on the town, remember? We're going to enjoy our dinner and the theater."

"You're hurting, Lora. That's more important."

She sat up straight, put the shell from her last shrimp on the pile with the others, and assured him. "I'm fine, Michael. Really. I appreciate your concern, but right now what's important is that I'm nearly finished and you still have half of your salad and at least a third of your shrimp to eat." She laughed both at her own dilemma and the ridiculous expression on his face.

As it turned out, they decided it would be best not to get

dessert but to drive to Swope Park as soon as they'd finished their meal. With fifteen minutes until the orchestra's overture, the nearby parking areas were already filled, so they were directed to park with hundreds of other vehicles on the grass-covered hillsides. The evening was still very warm but the stifling humidity had let up.

Lora and Michael were amazed that hundreds of people were still arriving and that there was adequate seating for them all. The woman taking their tickets appreciated their comments. "We're proud of our Starlight Theater. Did you know it's the second largest outdoor amphitheater in the country?"

Huge turrets graced the outer sides of the brick-faced stage wings and vaulted archways marked off the sides and back of the area in which were the thousands of theater-type seats. "It's sure a lot different from the auditorium in my high school. Did I tell you I once played Professor Higgins?" Michael slyly asked.

"And I was Eliza Doolittle for a little theater production during college!" She was looking at the program. "I trust we won't mortify one another by bursting into song when they get to our favorite numbers."

He was delighted at the thought. "Which favorite shall I anticipate hearing from you?"

"No question about that." And she began to sing softly, but with a flair and verve that showed how good she'd undoubtedly been. " 'I could have danced all night, I could have danced all night, and still . . .' "

She noticed the smiles of some sitting nearby and her former reckless abandon and joy changed to profound embarrassment. She sank down into her seat, her hands clasped sedately on her lap. "Now it's your turn. Which of your numbers would you pick?"

"Also no question, the recitative of Professor Higgins: " 'I've Grown Accustomed to Her Face.' "

"I like that also. Especially because of the reason he sings it, his fear of vulnerability, of admitting he's fallen in love with her."

After the instruments were tuned, the grand strains of the magnificent score were heard. He leaned over to whisper, "Did you have difficulty learning the cockney dialect?"

She nodded. "That was the hardest part of all, especially when being taught onstage to unlearn it."

He remembered vividly. "MariLee, the girl who always got all the leads, was awful with that. It wasn't until the last week of rehearsal that we had any reason to hope for the show's success."

"They didn't consider replacing her?"

"Hardly! Her father was the supervising principal. She didn't volunteer to step down and the director didn't have the nerve to make her do so, though some us threatened mutiny."

"What happened?"

"I've wondered already just what did take place behind the scenes or whose idea it was, but someone came over from the speech or drama department at the university and gave her private lessons. And MariLee ended up doing a commendable job after all."

Neither of them actually sang along with the talented stars, but he heard her humming a number of songs, and caught himself doing likewise. He was intrigued by the skill and rapidity of the many scene changes and thought of the uncounted hours he'd spent helping the properties figuring how to make them work better.

It was intermission. "Popcorn time!" Lora announced, jumping to her feet. "I get to buy it 'cause I thought of it first."

"I never heard of that rule," he protested, following her to the aisle. "It must be a fairly new one."

"About as new as any can be," she agreed.

"Like about thirty seconds old?"

She looked back over her shoulder, her blue eyes sparkling. "About that." They carried their snacks with them along some pathways, not talking much, but comfortable together. That was something he'd noted while riding with her, something which had not happened to him very often when he'd dated. Lora did not need to fill the silences with words.

The second half went even more rapidly than the first. *Was it the play itself or his companion who made this evening so enjoyable, so exceptional?* Michael wondered. He closed his eyes for a moment as he considered that, and opened them immediately as his arm was elbowed sharply. "You should be ashamed of yourself! Bringing me to a play and then going to sleep. You have no idea what that does to a woman's self-esteem!"

He smiled, at peace and content with himself and her. "I was savoring the song and the evening and the woman beside me. Believe me, Lora, your ego has nothing to fear from me this night or any night or day."

The laughter in her eyes and on her face changed to something totally different, more intense, yet insecure. Her eyes turned quickly away from his, finally focusing on her own hands clasping one another so tightly her knuckles looked white. "Oh. Well . . . thank you."

knuckles looked white. "Oh. Well . . . thank you."

He reached to cover her hands with his. "You have nothing to fear from me, Lora. I promise you that."

Her head tilted forward slightly and it was her turn to sit for a moment with eyes closed. Michael noticed her chin was trembling as Abbie's did before she'd burst into tears. With Lora, however, he couldn't just draw her into the safety and comfort of his arms.

I shouldn't have come with him! I should have made some excuse or insisted on staying with Phyl tonight or something. I'm too weak to handle this. . . . She moved her hands under his, determined to release them, yet treasuring their warmth and protection.

She sat up taller in her seat but slanted a little away from him. She must say something. "I especially like this one, don't you?" she asked, even while realizing she would have said the same thing about any song being presented at that moment.

"Yes. I do."

She forced herself to pay attention to the stage only, and she was pleased at how many of the speeches she remembered word for word. Driving through Kansas City on their way back to the motel, she commented on that as well as his traffic savvy. He was obviously more used to maneuvering through city traffic than she.

She did not feel threatened until he asked her opinion of the last scene of the play. "I'm not quite sure," she began. "I'm glad Eliza decides to go back. And I'm pleased he realizes he loves her. But I'm not positive it's established that, though she's willing to bring his slippers (which he doesn't deserve, incidentally), he's going to give her the respect and consideration she requires."

They must have driven a full block before he asked, "Would you have brought the slippers, Lora?"

They were halfway through the next block before she answered. "I'm afraid I would have. . . ."

eight

Even before Lora opened her eyes to look at the alarm clock she remembered she was in Kansas City and would have this day free to spend as she chose.

As she chose. What wonderful words they were, and how seldom she'd been able to say them! She was smiling as she stretched to her full length in the queen-size bed then snuggled again under the sheet, the only covering she'd needed throughout the summer night.

Seven-fifteen. Sunday morning. She could luxuriate in the laziness of sleeping in or, more likely, of just lying here thinking or dreaming or considering the what ifs of her life.

Last night had been so wonderful! She'd spent it with a marvelous man who had enjoyed their time together as much as she, that is unless he was as good an actor in real life as he'd probably been in his high school play. She could not conceive of his being anything but successful at anything he tried.

How awful it must have been for him to have lost his young wife! Even with his mother's help, the stresses of raising two children in addition to running an interstate business must be monumental. But he did not complain.

By contrast, he knew she was unhappy about things in her life. Furthermore, he had to realize she was a woman who couldn't cope with what life handed her or she'd still be at her old job at the hospital. Sighing deeply, Lora pushed herself up to sit on the edge of the bed, her fingers running back through her hair as her feet felt for slippers.

A shower would make her feel better, but she stopped halfway there to consider this most recent mood swing. She had been blissfully happy when thinking of Michael but in the dumps when dwelling upon herself.

You have a problem, Lora, she berated herself. *A big one. A week ago you didn't even know this man, and now you're worrying about whether he thinks you're a sniveling weakling! Well, enough's enough!* She wasn't so different from Sally after all, she told herself.

She usually had her devotional time before getting out of bed in the morning, but on this day she was fully dressed and ready to leave before reading several Psalms and praying. She hoped this was good, making herself more attuned to God shortly before attending services in His house.

This Sunday she would be in God's house! She thrilled to the thought as her only choice when staying with Sally was which preacher to watch on television. Her sister did not like the programs she preferred, but Lora had learned that by making an effort she could still get something from the messages.

There was a knock on the door and Lora welcomed Michael. Glancing at her watch, she accused, "You must have walked up and down the hall waiting for exactly eight forty-five."

He smiled. "I didn't want to rush you."

She took his arm and matched his steps toward the exit. "I do hope you had a good night and that today will be all you want it to be."

She glanced up questioningly at his unreadable face. When they went for breakfast at the same restaurant as the previous morning they spoke mostly of the show the night before and of the weather which was overcast and appeared threatening.

She worried a little at his silences but she had no right to ask questions. Later, as they parked at the hospital, he reached out to put a hand on hers as she was about to open her door. "Lora?"

His serious tone was ominous. "What is it, Michael?"

"I . . . got a call early this morning. From Betty. Her daughter's in the hospital with an ectopic pregnancy. She has two small children and her husband has to be away much of the time. Betty is leaving for Philadelphia to take care of everyone."

"Oh, I'm sorry. Is she all right?"

"She's had surgery during the night and seems to be doing well."

Lora felt a pressure in her chest and there was a burning in the back of her eyes. "So you will be flying back right away to take care of things at the office." It was not a question.

"Yes." His hand clasped hers tightly. "You'll get back the privacy of your cab earlier than expected."

"I. . . ." She wanted to say how much she'd miss him, but that wouldn't do. "I think our time together went better than either of us expected. You are an interesting man."

There was that funny little quirk at the right side of his mouth. "Interesting?"

If she continued to meet his gaze, she was afraid he'd read too much there. "I enjoyed our conversations and . . . appreciate all your help when I needed it. And your saving me even when it meant that your arm got hurt. . . ."

"I don't want to go, not right now. I should let Tony know when we see him. This . . . isn't the way I'd choose to say this."

She was thankful he hadn't planned things this way.

"When is your flight?"

"I wanted to go late in the afternoon, but couldn't make connections. I leave at one fifty-seven."

The only way she could get around this emptiness, this sense of loss, was to force humor. "I must say this is an original way of getting out of taking me to the zoo this afternoon."

"I'd looked forward to that," he stated, his face showing he hated to miss it. "And the only way I could take you for our white-linen-tablecloth dinner would be to skip church."

She enclosed his hand between both of hers and her voice was husky. "I'd really prefer our going to church together."

His smile was warmly comforting. "I thought you'd say that. I'm glad."

Michael held her hand as they crossed the parking lot and entered the hospital. There were many things he'd like to say to her, yet he was almost tongue-tied by his emotions. The few words exchanged sounded strained even to him.

Phyl was in the same seat where they'd found her before. "Hello," she greeted them with a big smile as she started to get up.

Lora entered the room in front of Michael and indicated that the other woman should remain seated. "We thought we'd visit before going to church. How's Tony doing?"

"He had a much better night, he says. And he certainly seems better." She looked toward Michael then back to Lora. "He has all sorts of questions as to what happened to his load and what you two did on Friday, so I'd appreciate both of you going in for this next visiting time."

Michael wondered if something, maybe a blood clot, had caused Tony to forget what they'd told him, but Lora explained it wasn't unusual for a patient with a massive heart attack not to remember clearly things taking place or being said at that time. Together they went over everything again for him from when he called to tell Lora he wasn't feeling good.

He gave her a long look of admiration. "Lora, I had no idea you could drive my truck."

"It was prayer and the help of the other drivers that gave me needed confidence. I had to get the load off the road, and it was even more essential to get medical attention for you at the rest stop. It was the only way I knew to accomplish both goals."

"But how did you know what to do?"

She looked embarrassed, as though they might not approve. "Well, sometimes as I was escorting I wondered what I'd do if there should be an emergency situation. And so I began asking questions of some of the drivers I went with, and they showed me the special equipment. One of the men left this work to teach driving and he arranged for me to take classes when I could fit them into my schedule. I did pretty well, except I need a lot more practice with backing."

They talked of other things until it was time to leave. Michael said, "Tony, I've appreciated getting to know you, and to learn how you and the other drivers look out for one another and for the escorts. I'm not sure I'll get to see you again, but I'd sure like to."

"Hey, Michael! I'm gonna lick this thing and be around for a long time. You'll see."

Michael grinned. "You'd better. After everything that's taken place thus far, you have no right not to hang in there." But then he told of his leaving in the early afternoon.

"What about you, Lora?"

Tony had already paired them, and Michael wasn't surprised by Lora's quick recovery. "I'll be starting out early in the morning to escort a driver going to North Carolina. Perhaps I'll get a load northward from there." She looked across the bed at Michael. "That shouldn't be too much to ask, should it?"

He wished he could assure her of this. "It's not too much to ask, Lora, and you'll get it if it can possibly be arranged. But you know I can't promise."

She was contrite. "I know. And I shouldn't tease."

Tony had been holding onto their hands and now drew them even closer. "You're going to think this a crazy question and I probably shouldn't be asking it. . . ."

"It's all right, Tony," she encouraged. "Ask anything."

"Well, I was wondering, and I know it sounds like I'm out in left field, but I have to know. Did you hear any . . . singing out there on the road?"

Her face blanched a little. "What kind of singing, Tony?"

"Maybe an angel. Or someone. I know my radio wasn't on but I heard singing about Jesus loving me and wanting to heal me, something like that."

Michael caught her quick glance and nodded. She stayed as she was for a moment, apparently trying to decide what was best. Then she leaned toward him and began singing softly yet with deep meaning "Jesus Loves Me."

Tony's face lit up and he started to sing with her, having to wait for her to form first those words she'd altered when singing to him. "Was there—it seems as though the voice—you—called me by name. Was I fantasizing?"

She reassured him, "It was the second verse: 'Jesus loves you, He will stay, Close beside you all the way. Tony, He wants me to say He is with you here today.' Is that how you remember it?"

He nodded, his eyes moist. "I also received orders to keep my heart working, right? That may be why I'm here, or at least it's some of it. I remember I was running through a long tunnel with a light up ahead. I got close to the end and the light got even brighter, like on the very clearest of days. And then I heard your song. I didn't know where it was coming from, but it seemed like it was drawing me back. Making me want to need to return to my wife and kids and friends, and everything."

"So you did," Michael said.

The dark eyes met Michael's. "I did, and for a while there after I came to I had doubts about how wise I'd been. I kept remembering my eagerness to get to the light and if I'd done that I wouldn't be having that excruciating pain."

Lora raised his hand and placed it against her cheek. "I'm sorry about the pain. I wish I could have helped."

"You did. More than you'll ever know. . . ."

As they walked to the truck Michael said, "This is totally selfish, but I'm glad Phyl decided to go to the service in the hospital's chapel instead of accepting your offer to join us."

"I had to ask."

He squeezed her hand. "It was the right thing to do. She probably should have come, to get away from the hospital and motel."

Once inside their church of choice this morning, Lora looked around at the tall, clear, stained-glass windows that gave a bright airiness to the wide, covered passageway around the entire rear of the sanctuary. People were talking and visiting, many drinking orange juice, tea, or coffee. Upon recognizing the strangers in their midst, a young man helped Michael and Lora get tea and visited with them.

Joining those entering the sanctuary. Michael was pleased when Lora asked if he'd mind sitting near the front, even if it would take longer to leave afterward. She bowed in prayer and he did likewise. Hopefully he wondered if her prayer might have included a request about him.

The organ prelude by Bach reverberated through the massive pipes that provided the backdrop for the thirty-eight-member choir. The pastor, a tall, athletic-looking man with a delightful bent for storytelling, appeared to be in his midforties. In addition to the excellent sermon, Michael stated afterward that he appreciated that portion of the service when two babies and their parents were dedicated to God.

Lora agreed wholeheartedly. "It was so sensibly specific, emphasizing the parents' promise to raise children as God desires. Never having had a child, I can only imagine what an awesome responsibility that must be!"

"It is. I well remember when Chrissie and I went forward with Abbie and then again with Chuck." For a few moments he walked in silence, obviously transported back to those days.

"I'd accepted Jesus as my Savior and was baptized when in my early teens, but it was with the birth of Abbie and knowing we wanted her to be raised in a Christian home that I came to grips with making God the Lord of my life. Does that make sense?"

She nodded. "Very much. I was baptized as an infant and confirmed at twelve. However, I didn't reach the point of wholehearted commitment until the end of my freshman year at Penn State. My roommate was a professing atheist and I tried witnessing to her, only to find that my own relationship with Jesus wasn't very strong.

"It took almost a year of intense study and prayer, and being open to the help of my pastor and a dear friend who was a Sunday school teacher."

She looked up at him with her clear blue eyes and added, "In some things I seem to be a very slow learner."

"I too. And unfortunately it's often in matters of most importance, isn't it?" She nodded and they continued walking across the parking lot.

"Lora," he said slowly, "I know we haven't known one another very long. . . ." He came to a standstill, so she stopped also, facing him. "If there's ever anything I can do, would you be open enough to let me help you?"

"I . . . don't know if I can, Michael. There's been so much in my life that I've had to handle alone that it's difficult for me to ask for favors."

"I don't mean to grant you favors, Lora. I care for you and would like to do what I can to help."

Her downcast gaze now seemed directed at his shoes. "You already have enough responsibilities with your business and your daughter and son, Michael. You don't need to reach out for more. With your mother leaving, you'll have even more to do for Abbie and Chuck. Knowing you, you'll be doing everything right in that department."

Drawing in a deep breath, he said, "It's impossible to always be right in everything involved with child raising, but I'll try to fulfill my promises."

"I'm sure you will."

He sighed. "That's why going home today is what I should be doing."

"And taking care of the office."

"Office responsibilities are why I have to go. The children are why I should be there. I'd planned to be home by Friday at the latest."

"Oh."

He wondered what she was thinking or feeling. "Much happened to change that."

"Yes." She then added quickly, "You were as concerned as I with Tony's condition."

He had the keys in his hand but didn't immediately unlock the door. "That's true but you must know by now, Lora, that I also wanted—needed—to get to know you better. I didn't choose to leave you on Friday or Saturday or today and would probably have stayed through at least the beginning of your trip east if Betty's daughter weren't having trouble."

Her face was radiant for so brief a time he wondered if his desire to see this response could have conjured it into his awareness. "Perhaps it's for the best that you got this summons."

"Don't say that! I have to see you when you get back. I want you to get to know my children and my mother. And I want to meet your mother and sister."

He had been drawing her closer until her cheek was against his, but she remained there for only a moment. "I'd like to meet your family, Michael," she admitted, "but it's probably best for both of us if that doesn't take place."

He tried convincing her but she was immovable. Finally he resigned himself to speaking of the sermon and of Tony, both evidently "safe" subjects. He then apologized for the necessity of returning to the motel for his luggage. He had wanted just the right moment to tell her he was leaving.

He'd done miserably with that. For that matter much of what he'd tried had not gone well.

Lora went with him to return his key and take care of motel

fees. She hadn't been sure whether to go to the driver's side when they got to the truck, but he'd led her to the other, unlocked the door, and helped her in. She smiled, liking the easy gentlemanly way with which he did things.

"Thank you, Michael."

His look was unfathomable. "You're welcome, Lora. For whatever you're thanking me."

Her head tilted slightly as she considered why she was thankful. "For being you," she said softly and looked down as she fumbled with her seatbelt. His hand remained on her arm and she was sure he was waiting for her to say more. What she had put into words could be interpreted more strongly than she'd meant, though not nearly as much as she felt. He sighed and closed her door.

Before leaving the truck at the airport, Lora insisted on re- bandaging his wound for a final time. She pronounced it to be healing nicely. She did not look into his face as she cleaned it with peroxide and secured in place the clean white gauze covering with tape.

After replacing excess supplies in the kit she lightly placed her hand upon the bandage. There were no words to her prayer, but it was a blessing. "I don't know how to thank you for protecting me like you did, Michael, even at the cost of your being injured instead of me."

"I do."

Her eyes lifted to his. "What?"

"You can thank me by letting me take you for that promised dinner as soon as you get home."

She did not argue, but she didn't agree, either. "We'll see, Michael. We'll wait and see."

After his luggage was tagged and started through its

channels, they decided to grab a bite at an airport concession. He did most of the talking, but she tried to answer correctly. She felt numb. There had to be many things to talk about but she could think of none. *How she'd regret this after he was gone,* she thought ruefully.

After he was gone. Four little words. Five small syllables robbing her happiness. Well, she wouldn't let that happen yet, anyway. "Do Abbie and Chuck know you're coming?"

He laughed, brown eyes sparkling, happy in the love of his children. "Abbie answered the phone this morning, but I talked with Chuck too. They're delighted to be coming to the airport and to pick up their old dad."

"Do they often see you off or come get you?"

"Not as frequently as they'd like. For most business trips I drive to the airport and leave the car. I'll undoubtedly take them up to the dining room overlooking the airport and they can watch planes coming and going while they have something to eat and we debrief one another."

He had that little crooked smile she'd come to love as he leaned forward, left elbow on the table, chin on his fist. "What shall I tell them about you, Lora, you who made this trip so unforgettable?"

She laid down her fork. There were little, tingly, prickly sensations running along her hairline but she would not release her hands clamped so tightly together. "Probably the less said the better. They would hardly be interested in hearing of someone they don't know."

"I can assure you my *mother* would be interested."

He might be teasing, though it didn't look or sound that way. "She doesn't know you've been traveling with a woman all week?"

He shook his head. "I didn't mention that possibility ahead of time as I wasn't sure you'd agree to my accompanying you. And, later, it wasn't something I wanted to tell about over the phone."

"Ashamed of me, boss?" she asked, deciding to take her turn at teasing.

"You know better than that, Lora. And I suspect you didn't mention me to Sally and your mother, did you?"

She felt a red flush grow on her face. "Guilty as charged. If I had, I'd still be on the phone trying to explain myself and our relationship, our business relationship, that is."

The first announcement was made over the speaker system that Michael's plane would soon be loading, so they went to sit together near his gate. A mother had difficulty controlling her three preschool children, a grandfatherly person was visibly fretting for fear he wasn't hearing correctly the loudspeaker-garbled messages, and members of families and groups were exchanging hugs.

While waiting in line with him to have his ticket and seat assignment checked, Lora felt his arm go around her waist. "I don't want to leave you, Lora." As the line began to move, they clung ever closer to each other. All that was important in the world right then was that she was in his tight embrace, her arms were around his neck, their lips pressed blessedly together.

She was unaware of tears on her cheeks until she felt him gently brush them away with his thumbs, his hands cupped around her face. "Lora. My beautiful, wonderful Lora. . . ."

"I don't want you to leave me, either," she whispered. "God help me, I don't want you to go. . . ."

She was hardly conscious of his moving them both out of the line. She clung to him and they kissed again before he held her a few inches away and said, "It won't be long. I promise. I'll see you as soon as you get back."

She nodded, feeling numb all over. She watched him leave her, saw him turn back once and then again to wave, and she raised her arm to let him know she saw. She hardly noticed when someone dashing up at the last moment bumped into her as he got checked through. She moved woodenly to the plate glass window and watched as the plane backed away from the building, turned, and trundled down the marked-out pathway.

Some fragment of thought indicated this was a lovely day for his flight, and she said a little prayer of thanks and a big one for his safe journey.

She watched until the tiny speck that held Michael disappeared into the cloudless blue sky. He was gone. This man whom until six days ago she'd known only as a featureless voice on the phone and a name on her paycheck, this man whom she had not wanted to accompany her, was no longer here.

She had tried to keep from saying or doing anything that would jeopardize their status of employer-employee, a man and woman who, at most, might be friends. Now she'd told him she didn't want him to go. And she'd not only received his kisses but responded to them with all her heart.

Forlorn and lonely, she walked through the huge airport, out the self-opening sliding doors, to the parking area. It was comforting to be behind the wheel, and yet even that was no longer what it had been. Michael had for the past couple of days been sitting where she was now.

She must not cry; she would not. She would go on with her life as though he had never entered it, for there was little chance of their being able to manage a workable life together.

Not with Sally and Mother needing her. And two small children needing Michael.

But she was fantasizing! He hadn't asked her to be his wife. What did she really know about him anyway?

Lora, you have to get hold of yourself and shape up, she scolded. And then she prayed, *Dear Lord, You'll have to help me with this. I can't do it myself. . . .*

nine

Spying a grocery store on her way back to the motel, Lora went in to buy a hoagie, some granola bars, a container of milk, and several apples. She also bought a Sunday paper before looking over the small display of paperback books. Nothing there interested her.

After setting the milk in the provided ice bucket, then going to get ice at the end of the hallway, she changed into her pajamas. Nothing less than a fire would make her leave today.

She would not think of Michael, but her wayward eyes accidentally checked her watch and noted the time he probably landed, when he'd be greeted by his little ones with their hugs and kisses.

Stop it! she commanded. *You've got to get control of yourself. He's their father; they're entitled to all his love. All of his caresses and endearments. And you are not.*

Her errant thoughts recurred in spite of what was on television. Even the baseball games being shown, which before she'd have turned off with no hesitation, made her pause.

She moved on, scanning for something of interest. Failing in this, she clicked the button and the screen once again became blank.

A fleeting smile played over her lips. Right at the moment, she'd settle for her mind becoming as messageless as the TV. She poured herself a small glass of milk and drank it before piling pillows into a backrest.

She read more of the paper than she normally would to make the time pass. The mystery she had expected to watch turned out to be a rerun, which she then turned off, then back on again. It had been good and she could watch it again. She ate her sandwich, wishing it were not so similar to the ones shared with Michael yesterday.

Some time during the evening she remembered she could call Michael if she chose. Last winter he'd given her his home number when there was a problem with her run and he'd insisted she call in when the load was delivered and she was in her motel.

She felt like Linus with his blanket, secure in knowing she could make contact, even though she wouldn't. Tomorrow, after she and her new driver were through traveling for the day, she would phone the office.

Since Betty was away, she would probably talk to Michael. Would it be embarrassing to talk to him after their farewell at the airport? She shivered, but even as she pulled the sheet and a light blanket up above her waist, Lora knew it wasn't because of the temperature in the room.

She reached for her Bible on the stand between the beds and began reading the book of Ruth, a favorite of hers when younger. How lonely it must have been for the young Moabite widow in the land of her mother-in-law's people! How frightened she must have been at times. And yet the love she had for the older woman and for God had given her the courage to not only keep going but to earn the admiration and love of Boaz.

She pounded the very firm mattress just once with her clenched fist and then reached to turn off the light before trying to find a comfortable position. She had to acknowl-edge to herself that it wasn't the bed's fault that she was having trouble concentrating on her prayers and was awake for a long time.

A fitful sleep and her failure to set the alarm made Lora thankful she still had milk and the granola bars and fruit to eat before she was on her way to meet her new driver and load.

Jule (short for Julian) Timmons was about as different from Tony as he could be, a short, slouching, nervous type who did not seem at all pleased by having been assigned a woman escort. Lora had been through this before and today, oddly, she felt glad for it. Her need to prove her capability helped keep her mind focused on things other than last week.

Her call-in that evening went much more smoothly than anticipated, or feared. "Hi, Michael, it's Lora," she greeted when he answered.

"Hello, Lora. How are things with you?"

"Doing very well, thanks. The trip's been uneventful thus far, although I've drawn a driver who obviously thinks I must have an ulterior motive for doing a man's job."

He laughed. "After what I've seen of you, if you haven't already convinced him he's wrong, he's an idiot."

She smiled in the privacy of her motel room at his way of giving compliments. Quickly, however, she got down to the business of giving their routing and mileage and telling where she was staying, when they'd be leaving the next morning, and their expected time for offloading. "Have you found me a truck to escort north from there?" she asked hopefully.

"I think so, but the final details aren't worked out. Call from your first rest stop in the morning, or wait till you arrive. I should be able to tell you by then."

She heard a phone in the background and was not surprised at his asking her to hold a minute. And then he was on again, apologetically asking if he could call back in a few minutes as there was something he had to take care of right away.

"It's okay, Michael, I'm finished here. Anyway, I'll be going out to eat in a little while, so don't bother calling. I'll be in touch tomorrow."

"Lora. . . ."

It sounded as though he were about to protest or to plead and she couldn't handle that now. "Perhaps then you can tell me how you're coping without Betty and how her daughter's doing. Good night, Michael."

There was a pause before he said in a voice that was almost a sigh, "All right, Lora. I hope you also have a good night."

This was a better night than the previous one. She awoke refreshed, got around quickly, and was ready for breakfast when Jule came in from his truck. He seemed more accepting of her today and she wasn't too surprised when, as they separated after completing their mission, he shook her hand. "You did a good job, Lora, and I thank you. I've always been sorta glad not to get 'stuck' with a woman escort but if you're a typical one, I'll admit I was way off base."

Lora was still smiling when she went to the phone to call Michael. "Hi, Lora," he greeted her happily. "I'm taking the other phone off the hook so I won't be interrupted today."

She laughed. "How can you run a business like that?"

"At the moment, I really don't care. Not when I've been awaiting your call ever since midmorning."

"Well, we made only the briefest of stops. My driver wanted to get here as soon as possible."

"Did he shape up and realize what a gem he had with him?"

"He did shake my hand and indicate he wouldn't mind

having another woman escort, so I guess I served a purpose."

"Lora," he paused to clear his throat, "you always serve a purpose. And right now I have a purpose and that's to get you home as soon as possible."

"You've arranged for me to escort a truck northward?"

"I certainly have. Tomorrow morning at 7:30 you'll be expected at Dashiel Dynamics, at the Industrial Park in the northeastern end of town. Your driver is Ed Pulaski, out of Indianapolis. Do you know him?"

"I don't think so . . . I've never traveled with him. But I've been escorting enough now that sometimes I remeet somebody that one of my drivers knew or we'd eaten or had coffee with. That's always a nice surprise."

"You're always finding nice surprises in your life," he complimented.

"Not always, Michael, as you have reason to know." She was trying to be honest with him.

"Lora, I like you just the way you are, which is, by the way, much better than you give yourself credit for."

She hoped he had not thought she was fishing for compliments. She hated when other women did that sort of thing. It was time to divert the conversation. "I wanted to tell you that I called the hospital last night and they let me speak with Tony. Isn't that great?"

"Sure is. How's he doing?"

"He's been transferred to the fourth floor, to the unit where all the patients are taken following heart attacks or heart surgery. He's feeling good enough to grump about the salt-free diet and claim that the therapists insisting on his getting out of bed and walking are sadistic monsters."

Michael chuckled. "I can imagine his telling them that. But, really, it will be hard for him to change from ham, corned beef, eggs, and all the pies and other things he so likes to eat."

"He's determined to stick to it, though. He told me that later he'll be having a nuclear medicine stress test and other things to make sure, but the doctors believe his getting started so soon on the clot-busters may have kept him from any or much damage."

"Thanks to you!"

"And to you, Michael. I couldn't have done it without you." He started to protest but she overrode him. "You set up the flares and caution signs, brought the medical kit, rode escort for me, *and* gave me the courage to keep going."

"I gave you courage? I can't believe that, Lora. I wasn't exaggerating when I told Tony how scared I was!"

"You think I wasn't?"

"Of course you were, probably more than I. You knew, after all, how serious he was, while I could only guess. Your going ahead and doing what must be done shows much more courage than I could have mustered."

"Ya'know, we could get a pretty good mutual admiration society going here if we work at it," she teased.

"And the next meeting of this superb society will be held at the Hartfeld Inn at seven-thirty evening after next. The white linen tablecloths have been arranged in one of the private rooms and I've taken the privilege of ordering everything from appetizer to dessert."

She was thrilled but dismayed as well. "Michael, I can't go with you then."

"Have another date?"

"Hardly! I didn't even know I'd be home then."

"I'll pick you up at your house a little after seven."

"Michael! You're not listening. . . ."

"This dinner was agreed between us. I owe it to you."

"Then I forgive the debt. You see. . . ." How could she possibly explain this? "Sally and Mother would never forgive me if I just come home and then go out on a date, or whatever," she added, wishing she hadn't used that word.

"It's okay to call it that. And it's got to be okay for you to go out for dinner if you want to." Before she could respond he asked, "You do want to, don't you, Lora?"

His voice was as wistful as a child's and she didn't want to hurt his feelings. It had been so thoughtful of him to make these plans. "I couldn't on the first night back. They don't even know about you. . . ."

"And what will you tell them about me?" he asked.

She filled her lungs as deeply as possible and her voice was small. "I wasn't sure I'd be telling them anything."

"But now you're going to, right?"

"I—I guess I'll have to."

"That doesn't sound too complimentary, but I'll accept it," he said. "I'll change our dinner reservations for the same time the following evening."

That was the best she could do right now. After asking about his children and mother, she brought the conversation to a close. She knew, however, that the next day's call-in would not be any easier, nor less enjoyable.

Why couldn't she get this sensible head and foolish heart to work together for a change, instead of at cross purposes? Her thoughts would not be stilled nor her heart quieted, certainly not while confronting the progress of love.

Michael hung up both phones and leaned back in his leather office chair. He hadn't been sure she'd go to the restaurant with him even when he made those reservations. And now he'd learned she hadn't planned to tell her family about him! This was a blow that, thank God, had proved to be not as bad as he'd feared at first.

At least she hadn't questioned how he'd managed to get a northbound run for her from North Carolina. He'd rather not have to explain that he'd called in several favors to manage that. He'd also given up the run he should have asked Lora to make to southern Texas.

Lora was coming home! He got up and walked around his desk to the outer office where the young woman who'd come to work here two years before was sitting in front of the computer at Betty's desk. "Anything new or exciting?" he asked.

Celia gave him her usual bright smile. "Caulkins Express needs an escort from Trenton to near Nashville, so I've got Ned Kelly on that; Faberiron wants someone from Oshkosh to San Francisco and I'll ask Murph Henry to take that when he calls in; Henry Frankford will be taking the Biers Generators run from Seattle to North Florida; and I assume you got the okay from Lora on the one to Texas."

"Afraid not this time." He shook his head. "She has to get back to Pennsylvania, so I traded Kent Brigam their northbound trip for our western one." He tried to make that sound casual as he moved toward the filing cabinets.

"Anything I can get for you?" Celia asked, getting to her feet and moving toward him, her long pleated skirt swinging around her legs.

He motioned her back to the desk. It was fine having the attractive twenty-two year old here as long as Betty was also, but he always had the feeling she was trying overly hard for his attention. "No, thanks. I want to check a folder, and it's . . . right . . . here," he said, pulling it out and closing the drawer. He carried the file back to his desk, hoping she couldn't see what he'd taken from the personnel section.

Ah, yes. Lora Elizabeth Donnavan. Age twenty-six, almost twenty-seven, as of the thirtieth of next month. Born, raised, and educated in Pennsylvania. There it was, BS degree from Penn State, as she'd said, but no mention of what her degree was in. Reading on he discovered she'd done volunteer work at the hospital while a student, was a major caregiver for a handicapped relative (helped an uncle with his store), and enjoyed driving, gardening, cooking, sports, and children.

There was a picture. What was it, her high school graduation photo? She looked approximately that age, with big blue eyes looking into his, lips parted slightly as though about to speak, hair long and loose over her shoulders.

Although it was only wallet size, he held it with both hands. How young she was, innocent yet vibrant. *She hadn't changed much,* he thought. Her hair was now short and curlier, and she'd learned to be a little more careful about the expression in her eyes that showed . . . he wasn't sure what word fit . . . vulnerability?

He leaned back and stared up at the ceiling. Had Betty any idea how little of the essence of Lora Elizabeth Donnavan was recorded in this file? Had she deliberately left out information? If so, why? Had Lora asked this of her?

It was definitely a possibility, come to think of it. Lora had said she wasn't surprised that Betty had prayed for her when she'd continued on with that load that had to get to the dock in time to meet the westbound freighter. And Betty seemed to have a special fondness for the younger woman, manifested most clearly by her often trying to talk with her when she called.

Intriguing, that's what it was, he thought slyly.

He reached for the pad on which was written a number beside Betty's name. "In case you have to call . . ." were Betty's words, he believed.

Betty answered the phone and there was a lot of racket in the background. "Is something wrong?" she asked.

"Hey, isn't a guy allowed to make a call to see how his favorite and most important employee is making out?"

"Favorite and most important, indeed! I've been wondering about that. You were going to be back before the end of the week and something may have happened . . . ?"

He marveled at her astuteness once again. A widow in her sixties, Betty had been with him from the time he'd taken over the company. "Just what do you know about the young woman I rode with last week, Betty?"

"Quite a bit, actually."

"So?"

"She's a fine person, as I'm sure you've found out by now. She grew up in our church and I had her in Sunday school when she was in high school. Her father's dead and her mother, well, she's an emotional martyr, sacrificing herself first to a drunken husband and then to the tyranny of a daughter with multiple sclerosis.

"I was delighted when she went to become a nurse and hoped she'd get out of the home situation before her mother turned her into a junior copy of herself. What happened was almost as devastating: She tried to be everything to everybody, and almost crashed in the process."

"She told me she'd burned out from all the kids dying. . . ."

Betty sounded relieved. "I'm glad she was able to talk to

you about it. She definitely didn't want that information in her file. I hope she's come to terms with 'not being able to cope,' as she put it. She sounds better on the phone, but I seldom see her anymore, even at church."

"She is doing better, but still has a way to go. As for church, Sally insists on someone staying with her all the time. When Lora's home, she lets her mother go."

Michael then inquired about Betty's daughter. Tanya was at home, on very restricted activity, and Betty wasn't sure when she would return to the office. Pausing for a moment, he asked Celia if there was anything to be checked with Betty but was assured everything here was great.

By this time the hubbub in the background included screams and cries. "Sounds like they're in their 'Let's-drive-Grandma-crazy-while-she's-on-the-phone' mode."

She groaned. "I don't know what it is about having a caregiver on the phone that brings out the dickens in kids, but it's certainly become a major skill among today's children. I'm about to settle this dispute so, Michael, you take care of things there and give my love to Lora."

"I'll do that," he promised and winced as he cradled the phone. Lora would undoubtedly be more receptive to hearing of Betty's love than his.

Lora went directly home, planning to call in to the office when she got there. However, Sally was in a foul mood and began berating her from the time she walked through the door.

Sally's favored themes got their usual play: Lora did not care for her mother and sister at all; she was so involved with her personal life she couldn't even call and let them know where she was or what she was doing; and she was so self-centered that just because she had a truck and could wander off and do goodness-knows-what with anyone she met, she considered herself above the ethics and morals and plain consideration that makes civilization what it is.

Lora felt almost suffocated by the transition from being a respected member of society to being stabbed by flung, barbed insults. If only she knew how to react without setting Sally off on further tangents! She'd tried defending herself, ignoring Sally, and just being submissive, but nothing ever worked.

She spoke softly. "Sally, I came as soon as possible. Actually, I should be in Texas right now but I asked to come home. Please accept the fact that this is my job, and I have to be on the road to do it. . . ."

"But you shouldn't be doing this work. Not with your education and the pay you'd be getting and the security and everything."

She would have continued indefinitely along this theme had not Lora said firmly, "But this is my job. I have chosen to do this and intend to continue it. Is that clear?"

The harangue began again but this time Lora went to the side of the bed and leaned over the rail, her face only a foot away from her sister's. "Sally! I will not listen to any more of this. Do you understand that?"

"Who do you think you are, anyway? You go off whenever you choose and come back whenever the mood strikes. And we're supposed to wait and be grateful for any tidbits of attention you choose to give."

"You poor, miserable woman," Lora said, standing straight and shaking her head slowly. "You have never learned to be grateful for anything in your life. Were I not employed, there would not be money to maintain this house or pay the taxes and you would have long ago become a resident of a nursing home. Instead, I am holding down a job and you condemn me. You can't have it both ways, Sally."

The bedridden woman's mouth opened to speak and if the contortions of the face were any indication of what was to come, it would be further condemnation. Lora laid her hand over Sally's mouth to stop the words and immediately Sally's fingers, which were constantly curved inward now, probably from not getting exercise, came up to pull with surprising strength on Lora's hand and arm, the nails scraping her flesh.

"Think about it, Sally. Decide whether you want to stay in my house. Decide what you think the rules of members of this household should be. All the members of this household. Including you as well as Mom and me."

She left the bedside and went to the kitchen where the dishwasher was running and the radio blaring in counterpoint to Sally's loud TV in what used to be the dining room. "Hi, Mom," she greeted, crossing the linoleum floor to where the dusty blond woman was peeling potatoes at the sink. She looked far older than her sixty-odd years.

Her mother turned to kiss her cheek. "I didn't hear you come in, Lora. Will you stay a while this time?"

"I don't know yet. For one thing, Sally started right in on me when I came in. . . ."

"Poor Sally hasn't been in a very good mood lately."

"Mom, when was the last time 'poor Sally' was in a good mood? I can't remember any in the last year."

"Well, she gets upset that you're away so much. And you don't call very often, you know. . . ."

Lora reached for a glass from the cupboard to the left of the sink and headed for the refrigerator. "Honestly, Mom, if you were I and all you got was abuse when you called, would you phone very often?"

Elizabeth was defensive. "But we're concerned about you and want to know what's going on and that everything's all right."

Lora reached for the two-liter bottle of soda. "You may be concerned, but I've noticed something peculiar. The last several calls I've made neither of you has so much as asked how I was or what I was doing in my free time or anything at all about me except when I was coming back.

"I told you my driver had a heart attack and that I'd driven his huge, oversize truck into Kansas City, but not one comment was made as to my being able to do that. Neither of you asked whether Tony even survived, much less how he is."

Her mother was staring at her, wide-eyed. "What's gotten into you, Lora? You never talk this way!"

She sighed. "Perhaps I should have. Anyway, I just told Sally I wouldn't listen to any more of her derogatory remarks. And I also wanted her to be thinking about what rules we should be making for all the people in this household."

"Oh, Lora! That's cruel. You know how hard it is for her to be cooped up like this all the time."

Lora replaced the bottle in the refrigerator and eased the door closed with her hip. "Mom, she's cooped up because she chose to be. You know as well as I that she refused to cooperate with the therapists when they used to come. She wouldn't let us help her into the wheelchair and did not want to go outside, even when she was able to. She threw a fit or pretended to have palpitations or something when we tried forcing her to do anything she didn't want, which meant anything but watching those sick soap operas of hers."

"She also likes talk shows," Mom said, apparently still trying to defuse the situation.

Lora admitted, "Yes, she does. Those specializing in deviant topics or those on anything other than moral or family values. That's the only kind of show she's interested in, except for a couple of stupid game shows. She has a tantrum when I so much as want to watch the news or a public television documentary. Trying to be 'good old Lora,' I give in."

"That's nice of you, Lora."

She wasn't sure she was getting through at all. "I meant it to be nice, but I've been doing a lot of thinking while gone this time. I suspect neither of us has been kind to Sally by constantly giving in."

Elizabeth Donnavan's eyes filled with tears. "Don't you condemn me too. Sally's always telling me how unhelpful and unloving I am, but I try. I really do."

Lora set down her glass and went to put her arms around the older woman. "I know you do, Mom. And so do I. The trouble is, we're not making any progress as far as I can tell. In fact, she's getting worse."

"You noticed too. She's not able to do even as much as six months ago."

Lora had been referring to Sally's mental state but was willing to switch to the physical condition. "Neither you nor I can fully evaluate her. How much of her declining muscular ability is due to her refusal to do anything for herself? If she won't try, she can't do things. If she can't or won't do those, others deteriorate.

"I have no idea what level she could be brought back to if she'd make the effort. As it is, she's getting so bad that pretty soon she won't be able to do *anything* for herself."

"Lora, won't you please go back to work at the hospital?" Elizabeth Donnavan begged tearfully. "We could handle things, the two of us, if you weren't so stubborn."

It was always frustrating to try explaining their options. "I bought a book this week, Mom, and I've read the whole thing. It's on tough love and is largely about working with people who continually break the rules of the household, whether because of drugs, alcohol, personal problems, or just willful refusal to submit. I'd like you to read it."

"Oh, Lora, I don't have time or energy for reading. I'm so tired by the end of the day that I crawl in bed and collapse. And Sally has me up at least three or four times. . . ."

"For what, Mom?"

"All sorts of things. You know, rolling her over or getting her a drink or making her a sandwich or rubbing her legs when she has those muscle spasms."

"It's that often every night, now?" Sally had done this to her the last several times she'd been home, but Mom had not admitted to receiving the same treatment.

"Just about, yes. Sometimes more often than others."

Lora looked down at the back of her hand and arm where red welts had been raised. "Sally has much more control of her muscles than she wants us to know. Look at these marks she deliberately made with her fingers and nails.

"And notice how she gets herself into strange positions so we have to straighten her out. You wouldn't listen when I tried telling you last time about my setting up a mirror and watching her scrunch down in her bed and then call for me to pull her back up on her pillow."

"I still can't believe she'd do that!" Elizabeth protested. "Sally's too uncomfortable when she slides down like that."

"It may be uncomfortable, but it's an excellent way to get

attention. When did you last have to help her with this if you were continually in the room? It doesn't happen to me under that circumstance, but let me leave the room and I'll be called back within a few minutes."

"You're being unfair, Lora. She slides down during the night, too, and I have to help her."

"You sleep on your right side, with your back toward her, don't you?" Receiving a nod, she went on. "So you don't know if she gets bored or is angry with you or something. Maybe she's lonely, for all I know. Anyway, it's a way of getting you up and attending to her."

Lora noticed the loud sounds of the TV show suddenly decrease in volume and Sally's petulant voice calling, "I need help. I've slid down in this bed and can't get up."

Lora whispered, "See?"

"It's a . . . coincidence."

Lora raised her brows at her mother as she called, "Be with you shortly, Sally."

"I need help now!"

Mom started for the door but Lora touched her arm and reminded, "Tough love, Mom."

"But she needs me."

"Please, Mom, read the book. Then let's talk about it."

"I can't let her lie there all scrunched up."

Lora pushed herself away from the cupboard and went to the doorway. "Want some soda, Sally?" She raised her glass. "I just got some for myself."

"Sure I'd like some. But I need help here first!"

Lora turned away. "I'll be with you right away, Sally. I'll get your drink while I'm here and save a trip."

She tried to ignore the maledictions and comments about

laziness and lack of consideration as she poured from the bottle and replaced it. Mom had offered to go on in but Lora asked her not to, so she silently picked up another potato and her peeling knife, her ramrod back a silent reprimand.

Lora went to the bedside, set the glass on the stand, and, reaching across to put her arms around her sister, pulled toward the head of the bed. She then held the glass so the straw was in Sally's mouth and made small talk while the patient slowly sipped from it. Setting it back on the stand, she said, "I'm going to unpack now."

The volume of the television was back up to its previous level before Lora got to the doorway. She looked back and saw Sally, perfectly content, replacing the remote control beside herself.

ten

Michael frowned at the silent phone. Lora had still not called, although she must have arrived home several hours earlier. Of course, she might have tried when the lines were tied up, but she always rang again in that case.

He called the number that he'd been tempted to use an hour before when, at five-thirty, she'd still not made contact. The security agent wasn't able to give him the information he sought, but he was willing to pass on the call to someone else. Yes, the shipment from North Carolina had arrived during the afternoon. They knew nothing about the drivers of the truck or escort vehicle.

He wondered if there were any chance that Lora had shared information about him with her mother and sister. He started to punch in her number, but stopped in time. She had not originally intended to tell them about him. Even though she now planned to, presumably before their dinner tomorrow night, he had no reason to believe she'd done so yet.

So where did that leave him?

He'd better go home. He had called to say he would be late, that they should eat without him, but he always tried to have time with the kids in the evening. He wouldn't be home much tomorrow, if things went as he hoped.

They came running to meet him, Abbie with the coloring of her mother, Chuck so much like himself. He tossed them into the air, kissed them, and threw the Frisbee with them a while. Then placing one squealing child under each arm, he went into the house to greet his mother.

"Busy day, Michael?" she asked, smiling at him, her head still tilted upward from their affectionate kiss.

He set the children on their feet. "I'll be glad when Betty gets back. Celia and the others are doing a good job, but it's not the same."

She patted his shoulder. "Turnabout's fair play, as they say. She covered for you last week, you remember."

He stepped back a pace to look at her. "Must be date night. You look marvelous, woman!"

Petite with a size-ten figure, she looked stunning in an electric-blue sleeveless sheath dress. She twirled before him. "Can't have Sam losing interest at this stage in the game."

He grinned. "I know Sam well enough to guarantee he's much more interested in the product than the packaging."

"He is, indeed," came a drawling voice from the kitchen doorway and Michael strode over to shake hands with his future father-in-law. Sam was as tall and lean as Michael and, even with his prematurely white hair, looked much younger than sixty-four. His pink cheeks and light complexion contrasted pleasantly with Carolyn Harrington's darker coloring.

They visited for a short time before the couple left for a concert. After calling the office and finding there was still nothing from Lora on his voice mail, he asked the kids if they'd like to go out for ice cream. He went with them to the bathroom to wash their faces and hands and comb their hair before they raced for the car, Abbie winning, Chuck second, and Michael last.

"Daddy," Chuck announced at the edge of town, "you turned the wrong way for ice cream!"

"I thought we'd go to a different place tonight, okay?"

Chuck wasn't sure about that but Abbie felt adventurous

and convinced him this was a good idea. They sang songs and shared corny riddles and were unaware of the distance as their father drove the twelve miles to Belpark. They did know, however, that this white one-story house was not where they were expecting to get ice cream.

Michael held their hands as he started up the brick walk to the wide porch with its shallowly pitched ramp that could accommodate a wheelchair. Abbie's finger was poised over the button beside the door. "May I ring, Daddy?"

"Sure," he said as he looked around at the yard that had little shrubbery and only a few flowers. Neither Lora nor her mother probably had time for more than mowing, even though Lora enjoyed the beauty of growing things.

He heard her quick steps before he saw her through the screen door. "Hello," she greeted with what he considered a welcoming smile. Just then she noticed the children and stepped out onto the brick surfacing of the porch. "You must be Abbie and Chuck," she said, kneeling to bring herself to their size.

"Yes. We are," Abbie affirmed. "And we're going out for ice cream cones. Are you coming with us?"

The blue eyes seemed to be sparkling as they looked up toward him. "Am I?"

Bless that little daughter of mine! Michael thought happily. "We'd be delighted to have you join us."

She excused herself to reenter the house then turned back. "Is it okay if I go in my shorts like this or would you prefer my wearing jeans?"

She was asking him? "You look great as you are, Lora."

She gave him a flashing smile and he heard the murmur of her voice as she told of being invited by a friend and his children to go out for ice cream. He couldn't help but hear the resentful response. "You just got home, Lora! Can't you even stay home one night before ramming off again?"

She tried to say something but was cut off with, "Who is he, one of your truck drivers?"

"No, Sally, not a truck driver, though I know some fine ones," Lora said quietly and Michael could guess how she must feel about this kind of snobbishness.

Suddenly Lora was back at the door, drawing all three of them into the hallway. Slowly they approached the attractive, slightly overweight blond woman lying on a hospital bed across the room from the archway. Aside from that one piece of utilitarian furniture and a bedside table, the room looked like a normal, attractive, family room with its wide-screen television, comfortable looking tapestry-covered couch and recliner, and several fine pieces of walnut furniture.

Lora asked her mother to come in from the kitchen, off to the right, and Michael was introduced to them as the man who owned and managed the company for which she worked. Chuck immediately wanted to know what sort of a bed this was and how it worked and both of the kids were invited up onto it as Sally showed them how the electric controls operated.

"You wanna come, too?" Chuck invited when they were about to leave a few minutes later.

Sally rumpled his blond hair. "I wish I could, Chuck. But I can't."

"Oh. Well, we'll see you soon, okay?"

"Will you come back to see me?" Sally asked.

"Oh, sure. When Daddy brings us. It's too far to walk," he explained solemnly.

When they got outside, Michael's gaze met Lora's over the heads of the children. "Sally's not what I expected."

"Sometimes she's not what I expect, either. You may have heard her when told I was leaving for a bit. That's her usual self, unfortunately." Lora looked puzzled. "I haven't seen her as she was with your little ones for a long time."

"Perhaps that's a key?"

"Perhaps. I've been praying for some breakthrough and even wondered whether getting a kitten or puppy for her might help. But I didn't, as it would be more work for Mom."

There was little opportunity for serious conversation as Abbie wanted to tell Lora about their trip to the firemen's carnival the week before and Chuck added to that, then gave highlights of the well-remembered week's visit to his uncle's farm, about which Michael had told her. Lora encouraged their conversation and told them of the mongrel puppy she'd been given when she was five years old. The easy give and take between Lora and Abbie and Chuck continued until once again they arrived at her doorstep.

An altogether perfect evening, Michael thought while getting ready for bed after reading the children's choice of books, including a chapter in a book of Bible stories. They had then prayed together, and he'd tucked them in with hugs and kisses. He'd had few expectations but much hope when deciding to go around to Lora's.

Thank you, Lord, oh, thank you! You've done it again . . . made something special out of what I almost feared to do. Please continue to help Lora with her problems and Sally and her mother. I also ask your blessings on Katie and Tony and all the others who especially need Your continuing care. . . .

Mom had already opened the couch and had it made up with fresh linens by Lora's return. Both she and Sally started asking questions, especially concerning how she'd come to know the boss so well that he'd bring his kids with him to ask her out. Lora had not yet decided how to explain Michael, but she now settled on a straight chronological account.

Sally got Lora up three times during the night and, despite her previous cross-examination of Lora, tried pumping again for further facts. Lora finally warned, "If you don't drop this right now, I'm going to my own bedroom to sleep."

When Sally persisted, still convinced Lora was hiding something, Lora gathered up her pillow and slippers and went down the hall to the end room on the right. It had been so long since she'd been able to use this room that had once been her haven. Exhausted, she collapsed onto the bed, not taking time to enjoy the cool blue and white color scheme, crocheted white bedspread and curtains, and built-in shelves loaded with treasured books.

Lora had threatened before to do this, but as she awakened and realized it was seven-thirty she could hardly believe Sally had permitted her a sleep of almost four hours.

She put on her robe and walked down the hall. Sally was sleeping, so Lora tiptoed to the kitchen and put water on to boil. Normally she'd have made her morning tea in the microwave, but this model had a beeper that couldn't be turned off, and Lora didn't want anything to disturb the sleep of either woman. She picked up a banana to take with her to the swing on the small back porch.

It was peaceful and quiet. Two purple finches were eating at the feeder and a hummingbird came to drink sugar water from the red dispenser on the porch.

When she was supervisor at the hospital she had bought this property and had many plans as to what perennials would be planted and where various herbs and trees would go. As things turned out, it had become necessary to hire a retired neighbor to do even the mowing. This took a sizable chunk from her already limited paycheck.

She leaned her head against the high back of the swing.

In spite of everything it was good to be home. It was especially so this time because of last evening and tonight.

She smiled lazily, thinking of what this evening might hold for her, for them. Then she heard Sally calling and got up from where she'd been slowly swinging back and forth, back and forth. She went inside, her day officially begun.

Today was better than expected. Neither she nor Sally apologized for what happened last night, but neither brought up the subject of Michael either. Mom seemed interested in the romance of his mother and was disappointed at Lora's not knowing more about that.

Mom looked better after her night's sleep, but Lora persuaded her to take an afternoon rest with the book she'd recommended. If reading made her sleepy, as she said, that would be fine also.

Lora gave her sister a shampoo, did some cleaning, and baked a chocolate cake while her mother went to the grocery store in the late afternoon.

She changed her mind three times before deciding on a sleeveless linen sheath the exact color of her eyes. Her choice was affirmed by Michael's admiring look. "I've sometimes wondered if my memory exaggerates how lovely you are, but you're real."

He came in to talk with the women for the few minutes they had before leaving for dinner. Samuel Schmidt was the man who would soon marry his mother, he informed Lora's mother. A fine man, one of the best, he added genuinely. He could well see why Lora's mother would remember him with admiration from years before when they'd been in high school together.

Her hand on Michael's arm, together they went down the walk toward the sparkling black BMW parked out front. "What a step down for you to ride all that way in my Nissan truck!" she said, fastening her seatbelt.

"You weren't supposed to say that," he reprimanded. "I almost brought a company car on the chance you'd feel that way, but I had such high hopes for you."

"That did sound like reverse snobbery, didn't it?" she said apologetically. "Well, I want you to know I'm fully enjoying this."

He reached to squeeze her hand, which he continued to hold as he maneuvered the vehicle smoothly. "Time is such a strange thing, Lora. It seems so long that I've been looking forward to being alone with you. And remembering our last moments together in Kansas City."

Her breath came in with a rush. She should look away from those warm brown eyes in which she could totally lose herself. But she didn't want to. She loved this man more than she'd ever loved anyone. . . .

Reluctantly, Michael turned his gaze back to the road. He was driving and there was no way he could continue to look into her eyes and not have an accident, in spite of all the TV shows and movies that show that very thing, she thought.

Hartfeld Inn proved to be an old, three-storied, many-gabled white building that had originally been a stop for stagecoaches. Its veranda, on which were a dozen or more comfortable-looking wooden rockers, went around the wide front and both sides.

They walked up the steps together and entered the large, majestically staircased foyer furnished with massive, marble-topped, carved walnut pieces. The hostess came to meet them and immediately took them down the high-ceilinged hallway to their reserved room.

Lora looked at the white-on-white embroidered linen tablecloth covering the single round pedestal table in front of a window hung with heavy, Irish lace draperies. The wall coverings looked like some she'd seen at Williamsburg and the chests and chairs were similar to those in the foyer. A large oriental rug graced the pine floor and two magnificent landscapes and a portrait had been hung artistically by their table.

She did not speak until the hostess lit the candles on their table and on the mantelpiece over the marble fireplace and left them. Lora's hands reached for his. "Magnificent, Michael. This is truly magnificent."

He raised her hands to his lips. "I hoped you'd like it."

"You knew I would," she said softly. "How could anyone not love it?"

He started to say something but saw or felt the marks on her hand and arm. "Lora! What happened?" The fingertips of his right hand caressed them gently.

She wished their closeness of a moment before could have continued but knew it was better that something, even this, had broken the spell. She told of what had taken place the night before with Sally and the conversation with her mother. She didn't spare herself as she confessed to going to her own bed during the night.

He was encouraging. "If she's able to do that to you, dear, it would seem she should still be able to respond to therapy. I think you're on the right track."

"I hope so," she said and was relieved when the waitress came with their shrimp cocktail. They became engrossed in trying to identify the ingredients of the special sauce.

Tea, fruit, and miniature hot sticky buns in a warmed bowl followed. The tossed salad was crisp and served with an iced house dressing that Lora surmised was similar to ranch but with grated cheese, pepper, and bacon. As she devoured the strip steak, which was fork tender and succulent, Lora sighed with satisfaction. "Kansas City may be known for its steaks, Michael, but these are the best I've had just about anywhere."

They spoke of many things throughout their meal, but by silent, mutual consent avoided anything depressing. Just before the baked alaska was brought for dessert he said, "I mustn't forget to give you a personal invitation from Abbie that I shall relay in her exact words: 'Say to her, "Please come here on Saturday and swim with us in the pool".' We hope you'll accept."

Lora had been afraid of this. She remembered the picture of Abbie poised on the diving board. Further, Michael had mentioned getting a tetanus shot after he hurt his hand when he was doing something to their pool. "I . . . don't know if I'll be free then," she hedged.

"I'd really like to have you there."

She shifted position on her seat. This was going to be more difficult than anticipated and she couldn't look at him. "Michael, I—I don't enjoy swimming. I'm sorry."

He did not respond until her eyes raised to his. "Then you don't have to swim, Lora. We'd still appreciate your being with us. Bring your bathing suit and lie in the sun. How long has it been since you've done that?"

"Many years. And I'd probably burn to a crisp, since I haven't even been playing volleyball or anything."

"No problem," he assured her. "We've got sunscreen of

every known protective capability, so you can take your pick. We'll even supply the beach towels."

She could feel the slow smile gradually growing as she sat there looking into his handsome face. "No wonder you're good at sales, Michael. But I hadn't bargained on a demonstration of your technique tonight."

He reached for her hand again and she shivered. "This has nothing to do with technique, Lora. I've never been more sincere in my life than in telling you that all of us want you with us. All day if you can, or whatever portion of the day you can share. You're under no obligation to swim unless you desire. Okay?"

She was troubled by not having been completely honest with him. What would he think if she told him she was absolutely terrified of swimming? But she didn't want to admit that as the pool must play a large role in their summer activities. She wanted with her whole heart to be with him and his delightful children. "Will your mother be swimming also?"

"I'm not sure what her plans are for the day," he said. "She's free of course to do anything she wants when I'm at home and is often with Sam or doing other things on Saturdays." His eyes showed the beginning of a smile. "Feeling the need of a chaperone?"

She raised her brows. "It's rather late in our acquaintanceship for that, isn't it?"

"It does seem that way, Lora." He was no longer smiling. "I think we did very well for the entire trip."

"Except perhaps at the airport."

"And yet that may have been necessary—as well as enjoyable—to make two conscientious yet loving people come to their senses."

"As you undoubtedly recall, I became a blubbering mass of femininity telling you I didn't want you to leave me. And then I was clinging to you and, and. . . ."

"You may finish your sentence, dear," he encouraged.

"I'm—I'm acting like an adolescent." Her voice was barely a whisper.

"No, you're acting like a woman in love. And I'm desperately hoping that's what you are, in love with me. Because Lora, I love you, I love you so much."

He had said the words. *Thank you, God! Thank you for his loving me and telling me so!* Lora could hardly keep her silent prayer to herself.

Yet there was Sally and her other responsibilities. And the children. How would they feel about this?

"Michael, I. . . ." She couldn't continue.

"Go on, darling. Please share with me how you feel."

"How I feel is the easy part. What we do about it is difficult."

Two little vertical lines appeared between his eyebrows. "Apparently saying what you feel is difficult, so let me help you. Do you love me, Lora?"

She looked into those intense, candle-lit, yearning eyes and was lost. She nodded her affirmation and then, when he still waited, she whispered, "Yes, Michael. I do love you, as I have loved no other."

His smile began slowly and gradually increased until, as he stood up and came around the table to her, his face was radiant. He knelt beside her chair and drew her to him.

eleven

She was like a doe coming to Michael's garden or a wren building its nest outside his door: not afraid of him, but of the unknown that might take place if she let him come too near. Michael rejoiced that she had managed to tell him she loved him, even though she turned her lips away so only their cheeks touched.

"Lora, my darling, my beloved." She was trembling in his arms. "It's all right, everything's all right now."

"But I'm not sure everything can be taken care of as we wish," she said. "I'm so afraid that something will happen, that I'll wake up and realize it was all a dream."

His body rocked a little as if reassuring or comforting one of his children. "God doesn't give guarantees, Lora. We've both learned that from experience. But He's promised to be with us always and that means this very moment, and tomorrow, and all through the future."

Her head tilted back enough so they could gaze into one another's eyes. "My soul knows that but my mind still looks for security, for permanence."

"Is marriage permanent enough for your mind's eye?" he asked. "Will you marry me and live with me and love me and accept my love and all I am, all I own, and all I'll ever be?"

She came to him then, her lips on his, sweet and yielding. He was filled with joy and happiness and a sense of deep, abiding peace more encompassing than any he'd felt since the death of Chrissie.

They finished their meal. They walked out of the old inn

and to his car. They drove together to her home and went up the walk and around the house as she led him to the porch swing. Awkwardly she put into words that she did want to marry him and that if it were all right with him, she'd like to consider herself engaged.

"If it's all right with me?" he repeated. "I've asked you to be my wife. That's what those words mean, my beloved, that we're really engaged, not that you consider yourself such."

She turned toward him, holding his hands almost convulsively. "I know, Michael. But it wouldn't be fair to you if I came as I am now, encumbered with cares and responsibilities that could keep me from being wholly, totally yours."

"You told me long ago—last week in the truck—that there's nobody else. . . ."

She pressed his hands to her lips then to her cheek. "That is the truth. It's my obligations to Mother and Sally— more precisely, my response to the obligations—that I must attend to. And dealing with my fears. . . ."

"We will work on these together."

"I wish we could. How I wish we could! But I've got to become stronger, to be worthy of being your wife and a mother to Abbie and Chuck."

He prayed for wisdom to help her, to get through to her, but no insights came. "It's strange, Lora, how differently we see you. You are one of the strongest women I know. No weakling would have patrolled Tony's load through the night when there was a chance something might happen. Your standing up to Ken to protect Katie took as much courage as anything I've ever seen."

"You have no idea how frightened I was inside."

"Of course you were. That's why I admired so much what you did."

He knew she wasn't convinced when she said, "Those were one-time things."

"You've been involved with trying to help Katie even after Ken's beastly nature must have worried you."

"She's my friend, and she needed help desperately. I had to be there for her."

"I, too, am your friend, as well as being the man who loves you. I need you and my children need you. Doesn't that count for anything?" He'd rarely begged for anything and had never thought he'd have to do it when he proposed. The alternative, however, was too painful to consider.

Her head was bent and he didn't know whether he had wounded her or if she might be praying. She drew in a long breath. The sliver of a moon gave little illumination but he knew she was pleading not only for herself but them. "You and your children mean everything to me, you know that. But because of that I've got to have some time. Please, Michael, give me time. It seems we've known each other much longer than we have. You've given me many insights, and many longings. I'd love to be part of a household like the one in which you grew up. I'd love to be part of your family. And I want—desperately—to be your wife."

He tried to draw her into his arms but she resisted. "Not yet, dear. I have to finish saying this. Somehow I've got needs and wants, responsibilities and responses, love and resentments, all kinds of things mixed up in me right now."

She stood up and he felt incredibly deprived as she walked away from him across the porch. But then she slowly returned and stood in front of him, hands behind her back in an unspoken request for him not to reach out for her. "Michael, could we for just a little while say nothing to anyone about our being engaged?"

One little spark of hurt flickered within him but he recognized this to be a manifestation of his male pride and squelched it. "I have feet of clay also, Lora." He stood up then but did not approach or touch her. "Your, our restrictions will allow us to continue seeing one another, won't they?"

She came to him, arms about him, lips raised to his. He held her close and kissed her, thinking this was her answer to his question. But then she said with an intensity that matched his own, "Oh, yes, my beloved. We must continue to do things together. I couldn't bear it if we couldn't!"

By mutual consent he left shortly after that and he wondered on his long drive home if he'd sleep much tonight. Would she? If she did not, would that be because of her love for him or because of Sally's demands?

"Since when do you take dates to the back of the house instead of bringing them in the front door?" Sally demanded as Lora entered the kitchen from the back porch.

Lora walked into what she now thought of as Sally's Room and laid her small purse on the chest beside the door. "It's such a lovely evening and you know I've always liked to swing. It seemed like a good idea to finish our conversation there instead of sitting in his car."

"What kind of car does he have?"

"A year-old black BMW. Very comfortable and smooth riding."

Sally's eyebrows shot upward. "Sounds like you've hit the jackpot with this one!"

"He's a fine man, Sally. It's a privilege to know him."

"What's his house like?" her mother wanted to know.

"I haven't seen it yet, but probably will on Saturday. The children have invited me. They apparently have a big pool and spend a lot of time outside."

"Did you tell them what a sissy you are where water's concerned?" Sally sneered.

Lora winced. "No, I didn't."

"Boy, are they in for a surprise! Are you going to get hysterical if you fall in or something?"

"Sally! That was a long time ago. How old was I—seven—when you threw me in, saying I'd get over it if my alternatives were to sink or swim?"

Sally laughed. "I had no idea you'd freak out. It was good the guy who owned the pool jumped in and fished you out."

It still wasn't funny to Lora. "I had nightmares about that for years." She felt that familiar shiver up her spine and turned toward her mother. "I've been wondering, Mom, do you know of any reason for my unreasoning fear? It's been with me as long as I remember."

A quick glance was exchanged between the other two women and Lora was certain that something had indeed happened. "Please, Mom, tell me. I've got to know."

Her mother laid down her knitting needles that were employed with creating yet another afghan. Every relative who'd been married for the last two decades had received one of these, as had people from church. Her tired face looked even more lined. "I . . . didn't realize you didn't remember."

"It's terribly important," she pleaded, moving in front of her mother, between her and Sally.

"I'm not sure just what did take place there at first," Elizabeth began. "Your father was having one of his many affairs, this time with a woman who was a real estate salesperson. She'd just sold a big mansion of a place and was ecstatic about her huge commission.

"For some reason she told him to bring his family to her celebration and Charlie insisted we had to go, though I didn't want to. He'd done the fixing up of the place, which had apparently helped make the sale, and she was showing him off, supposedly to help his business.

"The party started in the afternoon and by evening most people were showing effects of the unlimited alcohol. I wanted to take you home to bed—you were the only small child there— but Charlie wouldn't give me the keys and he became . . . abusive."

"How old was I?"

"Just three. You were a cute, friendly little mite who became quite the favorite of those retaining their faculties. Maybe that's one reason he wanted us to stay, your being such a hit, though it could have been because there was such a contrast between his successful new conquest and the dowdy wife he was stuck with."

Lora wondered which was more likely, but was impatient to learn more. "What happened?"

"Well, I had to go to the bathroom and made a point of asking your father to keep an eye on you for a few minutes. I wasn't gone very long, honestly I wasn't. . . ."

"I'm sure you weren't, Mom."

"When I came out of the house I saw all the activity at the pool." She paused, her face reflecting the horror of what she'd suspected, then seen. "I ran to the pool in time to see a young woman carrying what looked to be your lifeless body up the slope to the shallow end.

"A man lifted you out and laid you on the ground and worked with you for ages before you were able to breathe and move. Your first words were to call, 'Daddy! Daddy!' But he wasn't there."

Lora'a eyes closed and she bit her lower lip to still it. "In my nightmares I was always calling for him. It never made sense because I barely remember him except as someone lying on the couch yelling at me because I was doing something that interfered with his ball game."

Mom nodded. "He'd gone with his woman friend—and that's where someone found him—to get another drink."

Lora leaned over to put her arm around her mother's shoulder and kiss her cheek. "I'm so sorry for you."

Mom looked startled for a moment. "And I'm sorry for you, too. And for Sally."

Lora turned toward her sister. "You knew about this?"

"Oh, sure. I had just left for acting school in New York. Mom called and told me about it. I'd been angry with Dad before, and furious when he then threatened to leave her without a cent if she tried to kick him out."

"So he was in and out for that last year or two before he died," Mom finished.

"I'm glad it happened!" Sally said venomously, obviously referring to their father's death. "Especially when I got MS and had to come home. Can you imagine how awful it would be were he still here?"

Mom looked at her older daughter. "I wish you didn't hate him quite as much as you do, Sally."

"How can you say that? After all he did, you should despise him!"

"Sometimes I do, but not as often as I used to. He had a problem. . . ."

"More than one, Mom! Maybe he could have got help for his drinking if he'd wanted to. But his skirt chasing!"

Mom seemed to have shrunk down into the recliner. "Death is so final. While he was alive there was hope."

Lora looked with pity at this woman she'd thought of as her mother almost to the exclusion of her being a woman. *This conversation should have taken place years ago for the sake of all three wounded women,* Lora thought bitterly.

Even after her mother went to her room and Lora lay in the sofa-turned-bed, her mind went over and over what she'd learned. Her father had been a weak man, yet his passing had left his widow bereft of hope, his older daughter consumed by hatred, and Lora distraught with nightmares.

What other scars or weaknesses did she exhibit? What overcompensations had she made in her life? Was her own early childhood near-death experience what had triggered her desire to work in pediatric intensive care? Had her escape from drowning made her feel so strongly the necessity of pulling every other child back from the brink? Is that why she was so traumatized when she couldn't succeed?

Lora was still awake when Sally worked herself down in bed and called for Lora's help. Lora snapped on the overhead light. "Turn it off," Sally growled, covering her eyes. "You'll get me so wide awake I can't go back to sleep."

Lora walked across and leaned both arms on the railing of the hospital bed. "We're both thoroughly awake, Sally," she said quietly.

"Well, help me get straightened out then!"

"I don't think so, Sally. Not this time."

Sally moved her hand enough to glare at her. "What do you mean, 'not this time'? Come on, Lora. It's agony to lie in a twist like this."

"There are several good reasons for saying that, the major one being that you don't need my help."

"You're insane!"

"But not as crazy now as all this time I've let you use Mom and me. I've been suspicious for some time that you're capable of more than you let on. You can't feed yourself, but you maneuver the remote control and ruffle Chuck's hair and do this to my hand and arm," she added, showing the marks that were still there.

"You had your hand over my mouth," Sally cried. "What did you expect me to do, bite you?"

"The thing is, your hands—both of them—worked just fine to do your bidding. There was nothing weak about their coming up and slashing me like this."

"Well, maybe in the anger of the moment. . . ."

"And one day I fastened a mirror on the cupboard door and watched as you wriggled down in the bed so you could demand I come to help you."

A flush stained her face. "You rotten sneak! You just thought that's what you saw."

There was no point in arguing that. "Tonight I couldn't sleep after all the excitement. I was awake when you did the same thing a few minutes ago."

"You were having one of your nightmares again," she sneered. "Involving me, for some reason, instead of Dad."

"Come on, Sally. You and I both know what you're up to. I'm sorry you feel it's necessary to put on this act."

"You don't believe I have MS?"

"What I think is that you need to be evaluated. And it should be done soon."

"I went through all that years ago. You know what they said, that my condition will continue to deteriorate."

"But they also stressed that each case is different."

"Don't call me a case!" she cried. "I'm a person."

Lora laid her hand on Sally's hair. "I want to help you, but only in ways that will really help, not make you weaker and more dependent."

Sally glared through narrowed lids. "You think if you get me in an institution for testing they'll keep me there and you'll be freed up to do anything you please. But I'm on to your good works, sister, and it's not going to work."

Lora felt nauseated. "I'm asking you to think about it. Think about it very hard, Sally." She turned away. "And now I'm going to bed and I don't want you to even consider calling me for something like this again."

"Then I'll wake Mom," Sally threatened. "I need help right now to get back up on my pillow."

Lora turned back with a rueful smile. She would assist a hospital patient who acted like this, so she should do it here as well. She leaned over the bed rail to make the familiar lift. "I'm doing it this once, since you didn't know when you played your little game that you'd get caught. But I'm warning you, Sally, I'm going to be a lot more skeptical due to what's happened. Nothing is going to be as simple as before."

Sally tried another tactic. "What's with you anyway? Is it because of my making a joke about your being scared of water that you're set on destroying me?"

Lora was so tired. On this night that should have been the happiest of her life, the night when the finest, most loving man in the world had asked her to be his wife, most of her thoughts were on how exhausted she was and how she just wanted Sally to be quiet and let her sleep.

She returned to her bed. She prayed about Sally and about the relationship between the sisters and finally fell asleep thinking of Michael. Michael and his two dear children. Michael and Lora and Abbie and Chuck.

Saturday morning was cloudy and overcast. The weather forecasters had predicted "gradual clearing and sunny" and Michael hoped they were right. Lora had not said for sure she'd be coming and when he phoned Sally stated her sister wasn't there. Yes, she'd tell Lora he'd called.

There were many things to be taken care of around home even though he'd contracted for a student to do the mowing and trimming this year. He was sitting on the porch steps in the late morning repairing a wheel of Chuck's tricycle when the familiar Nissan stopped out front and Lora got out, calling, "Hi, everyone. I hope I'm not late."

With tools in both hands and the wheel held between his knees, he couldn't go to her at once and his called response was drowned by the children's squeals as they ran to greet her.

He twisted the final nut and set the vehicle on the walk. "Here you are, buddy," he said as he pushed it toward Chuck then walked the few steps to meet the woman he loved. He was relieved that, as she had kissed the children, she now raised her lips to him. Although her kisses for the three members of his family were all too similar, her smile for him was slow and sweet and held a special promise.

The most important thing was her having come. Of her own free will, she had come to him.

Before leaving for the day, his mother had prepared a vegetable platter and fruit salad to go with the hot dogs and hamburgers. Lora's potato chips and homemade chocolate chip cookies had to be put aside until the children finished at least some of the other food.

The sun finally burned through the haze and Abbie begged to be allowed in the pool, with Chuck echoing her request. Michael put them off for a while but finally sent them to put on their suits in the building at the far end of the blue-tiled oval pool. They were back almost immediately and jumping from the side and then from both the lower and the high diving boards.

"How did they ever learn to swim like that?" she asked, awed by their ability and their lack of fear.

"Their mother wanted to start them young," he explained. He'd decided that for someone like Lora it was essential to speak of his dead wife as openly as possible. "Chrissie began taking them to the YMCA's swimming classes when each was only six months old. They took to the water like ducks."

"Weren't you worried?" To Lora such a casual attitude was incomprehensible.

He called approval for his young daughter's particularly dramatic dive before answering the question. "I couldn't have taken Abbie myself, but I agreed it was a good idea since we already had this in-ground pool. Although we have a protective fence," he motioned with his arm toward the decorative redwood-and-steel enclosure, "and we keep the gate locked when an adult is not here with them, the best precaution is to have them be at home in the water and know how to swim."

She had tried to make him feel free to go in the pool with the children and she again asked, "Don't you want to put on your suit and join them?"

"Not if you're out here, my sweet," he assured her, but she didn't look convinced. "Is something troubling you, Lora?"

Her color deepened. "You're a dangerous man, my husband-to-be. At the very least, you'll keep me on the straight and narrow of truthfulness."

"Don't ever consider me dangerous. But as to the other, I am very interested in what you are going to be truthful about telling me now." He hoped his smile would let her know how much he wanted her to share with him.

She seemed to have difficulty determining what to say and he waited. She had to know by now that he'd be supportive.

She shifted position on the webbed recliner. "I told you I don't like swimming, Michael, when the truth is that I'm scared to death of water. For most of my life, this hasn't been a big problem, but you love it."

He seemed to expel a sigh of relief. "My dear, worrying, loving Lora," he said. "You don't ever have to swim if you don't want to. I realize the kids have been begging you to join them, but we'll explain about this and they'll accept it."

"I've had this, er, problem ever since I can remember," she managed. "It wasn't until last night that I learned why water frightens me so much."

"Would you tell me about it?" He needed to know, for her sake and for theirs.

She had been watching the children splashing with their inflated rings and toys. Her troubled gaze slowly returned to his and he saw the pain there as she spoke. It was when she told of the terrible nightmares that he moved to her recliner to rub her hands, cold in spite of the hot sunshine.

"Thank you, Lora," he said when she finished. He bent to kiss her. "Thanks for telling me. And I promise to try to be as open and honest with you as you've been with me."

She seemed to relax a bit as she put her legs over the side and stood. She was so near and yet, because of the restrictions she'd placed upon them and also because of the presence of his young children, he could not draw her to him and hold her. "I love you very much, my Lora."

Her hands clung to his. "And I love you."

The day went splendidly for Lora, even if she didn't go in the water. She even put on the one-piece blue swimsuit she'd bought on sale right after the Fourth of July. She had told herself she shouldn't spend this much money for something she might never wear, but now, seeing his approval, she was grateful for having made the purchase.

She helped Michael tuck Chuck in for his afternoon nap and then focused her attention on Abbie. Abbie was required to have an hour of quiet time during which she could color, look at a video, or have someone read to her. Lora was pleased to become the chosen reader and they sat together in a big, comfortable rocker in the airy living room.

She'd been surprised about the BMW and the blue-tiled pool; the white, century-old, vinyl-clad house was what she'd have expected. It was attractively decorated, but not in a way to call attention to individual pieces. The effect was of comfort and quiet good taste.

This was definitely a home. It was Michael's home. And soon it would be hers as well.

She looked up from reading a page and spontaneously smiled as she saw Michael enter from the kitchen. "Iced tea, possibly?" he asked in a stage whisper, raising the tall glass he was carrying. She nodded and he brought it to her before going to get one for himself.

Time passed rapidly. The others had assumed she would stay for the evening meal, but she explained Mom had planned something and she'd promised to be home.

As she was leaving, Lora asked if he had some runs for her. "Do you really want one right now?" he asked, puzzled.

"It is my job, you know. And it does pay the mortgage and other bills."

He nodded. "I'll call the office soon to see what is logged

on voice mail. So, would you prefer shorter or longer trips?"

"Either, although if I have my druthers, I'd choose to be home on weekends instead of in a motel." She quickly modified that statement. "Except for last weekend. I'd gladly accept a repeat of that if it could be arranged."

A sly wink was her goodbye for now.

twelve

She did need to get home to relieve Mom, but first she had made arrangements to stop at the home of Misty Tarnak, the hospital's head physical therapist.

The redhead was on her knees weeding a large, star-shaped flower bed in her front yard. "Don't let me stop you," Lora said as her friend started to strip off her gloves and get up. "We can talk fine while you work, Misty, and you probably don't get much time for this."

"I don't know why I bother with all these flowers," Misty grumbled. "As soon as I've taken care of each bed, it's time for another go around."

Lora admired the carefully manicured grounds. "You keep this place looking fabulous. I wish I had a green thumb."

"Don't even think that! It's a terrible taskmaster, and you have enough other responsibilities now with Sally."

"She's what I wanted to talk to you about."

Misty kept on weeding. "I hope I can help, Lora, but I'm not sure. You know she wouldn't do anything to cooperate when we tried working with her before."

"I remember all too well. However, there are additional factors now. Mom's having back trouble from moving Sally, and I'm away a lot."

"Still escorting?"

"Um-hmm. I enjoy doing it and it pays the bills. And I'm seeing a lot of America in the process."

"There are times I'm almost ready to chuck my work

too. Fortunately, just when we get several patients we can't seem to help much, we get breakthroughs (ease-throughs, more likely) with some we'd feared were hopeless. Also, it's not easy to give up what I've worked sixteen years to earn.

"But that's not what you came about," she said. Getting up, she removed her gloves and carried them with her as she led the way to the stone-pillared porch. They sat on wood-slatted rockers as Lora briefly explained the situation concerning her sister. "Of course you'd get a totally different picture were you asking Sally how she is. Maybe I'm unfair and she is almost as bad as she wants us to believe, but I don't think so."

"She doesn't know you're here, does she?"

"Not yet, but I'll tell her. What I need is input from you, a professional. Sally's afraid if she enters an institution for evaluation she may get kept there, and," her hands raised in front of her, then dropped, "I can understand her worrying about that.

"So I wondered, which of the doctors in your department would you recommend as the specialist to see her? It's got to be a relatively nonthreatening one, yet someone firm enough to hold her to whatever rehabilitation is considered necessary."

There was no hesitation. "Dr. Hinchmann's the guy for you. He's tall and young and, though dedicated to his work, teases and cajoles his patients into giving much more than they think possible."

Lora got the necessary information as to contacting the specialist and left, assuring Misty she'd let her know how they made out.

Sally went into a predictable rage at Lora's latest

efforts at her "rehabilitation." Mom was of little help. In desperation, Lora finally broke her own resolution and told of Michael's proposal.

"I am going to marry him," she stated. "And most of my time and energy will have to be spent taking care of him, two small children, and that home. I won't be here much of the time."

"Much of the time!" Sally cried. "You're gallivanting somewhere in that stupid truck of yours most of the time now. You're never here."

Lora didn't bother calculating for Sally the hours spent doing each of these, but again stressed Mom's worsening arthritis. How much longer could she do the lifting and turning, in addition to the bathing, feeding, and all the other things required for Sally's care and the managing of a house?

Lora continued pushing for at least one session with the rehabilitation specialist. "I'm praying he'll be able to come up with therapies to help you enough so you might be able to stay here," she said, deciding to be bluntly frank.

She saw Sally's wide-eyed doubletake. What was being offered was a possible alternative to leaving here, not the other way around. There was hot anger, even hatred, in her look before Sally pointedly turned onto her side, away from Lora.

Lora shook her head in frustrated sorrow, but then her shoulders raised and she almost smiled as she headed for the kitchen. She could handle what was meant as rejection. And she could handle being hated, at least for now.

In anger, Sally had just rolled over by herself! The

thought startled Lora and further cemented her determination. There seemed more and more hope for something to help her if she could only be motivated enough to try.

Lora had asked her mother to go to the early church service and even stay for Sunday school, if she'd come right home afterward. This would still give Lora the opportunity to attend the eleven o'clock worship service with Michael.

What made it most special today was being able to slide into the pew next to him. Abbie promptly switched positions so she could sit between them and was soon snuggling against Lora. Later, both children went forward for the children's sermon, then left for junior church.

This is almost like last week, she thought, then corrected herself. *I was so fearful things could never be the same between us once he left on the plane. Well, they aren't; they are exceedingly better.*

She involuntarily squeezed his hand. He returned the pressure and smiled. She doubted her answering smile appeared worshipful, but she did include in her prayers her heartfelt thankfulness. Afterward all four of them ate lunch at a nearby restaurant before she went home to relieve her mother.

Sally agreed to let Lora call on Monday morning for an appointment, and Lora saw her sister's disappointment when she learned that Misty had already tentatively signed her up for the next morning in a spot opened by a cancellation.

The next morning Lora helped the ambulance crew transfer Sally and the waiting began. It was a couple of hours before the nurse called to say Dr. Hinchmann would be giving Sally a preliminary report in about thirty minutes and her mother and sister were welcome to be present.

They arrived with time to spare, and were finally taken into the room where Sally lay. The rehabilitation specialist was very serious as he began giving his findings. He regretted that so much time had elapsed since she'd done much of anything. "This is going to make a comeback much more difficult," he explained.

"But not impossible."

Sally's effort to pin him down as to how much she might improve was countered by his asking how much she was willing to put forth and how much she wanted to be able to do. She snippily informed him that, in case he'd forgotten, she did have multiple sclerosis.

"I remember," he said and then smiled. "Incidentally, I don't care if you hate me much of the time here at the beginning while I'm giving instructions or assignments, Sally. However, we do have to set goals. I'm not about to set big ones as far as the world may see them, but reachable, serviceable ones.

"You will not only be relearning to lift your legs from the bed while you're lying down, but at the same time you'll be getting practice in sitting up more erectly and feeding yourself nonmessy foods. The therapists will have you moving balls or fitting objects together, things that will encourage manual dexterity.

"Some of these activities you'll think are boring and totally unnecessary. Do them anyway. Sometimes you'll be so tired you'll think you can't continue. Go on anyway. Sometimes you'll be sure we hate you and that we're downright sadistic. Trust us anyway."

He put his hand on her shoulder. His voice was soft but his message was clear: "If you don't, Sally, you'd better hope that the nursing home in which you spend many of your remaining years is a nice one."

Sally's face was white, whether from shock or antagonism Lora could only guess. She now joined in asking questions and received straight answers.

Yes, it would take a long time to see much progress. But Sally had not got in this fix within a short time either.

Yes, she must stay in the rehabilitation wing for her initial work, at least. They couldn't count on a ambulance crew being on hand to transport her to and from the hospital each morning and afternoon.

Yes, he anticipated it wouldn't take too long until she'd get around in a wheelchair and be able to take care of her own basic needs, "and hopefully much more than that," he added. But nobody could give promises timewise.

He'd checked with rehab and it looked as though they'd have room for her by the end of the week if that was satisfactory. Sally looked furious and frustrated but, surprisingly, did not refuse.

Betty was still not back, but the work was getting out on time and Celia was doing the scheduling quite well. Michael assured Betty of this when he called about an insurance matter, and she pretended hurt that he wasn't missing her at all. She said she'd better get back soon to save her job.

She showed up in the office the next day, saying her daughter insisted she could take care of things now with some help from a neighbor. Betty was delighted to learn that he and Lora were dating, but disappointed that she was asking to make some short runs.

"I thought, I hoped she might be willing to give this up if you two got serious," Betty confessed.

He wished he could tell her that he and Lora were engaged, but he didn't have that freedom.

"I just got home this afternoon for the first time since I saw you," Katie explained on the phone that evening. "I went through the messages on my machine and want to thank you for your help on the road and for your concern in calling so often."

Lora collapsed into a kitchen chair, weak with relief. "I've been so worried about you!"

"I'm sorry. I should have let you know I'm okay."

"Are you?"

"I think so."

"Anything new with Ken?"

"Well . . . yes." Her voice sounded uncertain. "After everything you've done to help me get away from him, I'm afraid you'll be upset with me. . . ."

What was it now? She tried to keep her voice from showing more than friendship. "Oh, I doubt that."

"You see, Ken did catch up with us at the next truck stop."

"Oh, Katie!"

"But he was under control by then and didn't object when my driver said the only way Ken could talk with me was in his presence."

"I would hope so."

"Ken did try to find out to whom the faxes were sent, just like you'd expected when you wouldn't tell me. But more important, he says he does believe in me, and he's offered to go for counseling."

They'd unsuccessfully tried to get him to do this before, but he'd always insisted nothing was wrong with him. Was he using this as a device simply to get her back? "Did you bring up that idea?"

"No, he did." She hesitated a moment. "Well, I said there was no point in trying again to live together, since the same thing always happened. And after he said he'd really try to control his words and actions, I said he might try but that I didn't think that could happen unless he had counseling.

"So then he said he'd go. If I went too."

"Did you agree?"

"I said I'd have to think about it and he came back home. I called him there several days later and told him if he'd set up an appointment with a reputable counselor, I'd try to arrange to be here for it.

"The appointment was at three-thirty this afternoon. I met Ken at Dr. Pennypacker's office and I think we've made a good beginning."

Lora supposed she should be happy for her friend but felt she needed to recommend caution. "You're not together now, are you?"

"I'm not willing to do that, and Dr. Pennypacker agrees. Not unless Ken gets straightened out."

"I'll continue to pray for you," Lora promised, thinking that with this change only God knew what was best for Katie.

There was a small pause. "Do that. The doctor feels I have a lot of straightening out to do also. He says I'm a codependent. My letting Ken get away with abusing me all that time is similar to what happens with spouses or families of drug addicts."

Lora had already told Katie this, but now Katie was at last receptive. "When's your next appointment?"

"Not for over a week. We made it for Friday afternoon, so I've asked my dispatcher to have me back in town for it. Ken did agree to go by himself, though, in case I can't make it. I think that's a good sign, don't you?"

"Yes, Katie, I do."

Time passed slowly in the Donnavan household. Lora checked on what Sally should take with her to the hospital and gave her mother money for several sweatsuits and pajamas.

Sally was not impressed by the outfits and ignored them.

Lora tried to help Elizabeth realize she shouldn't be disappointed. Sally was having as little communication with her family as possible, considering that they were the ones who bathed, turned, combed, and fed her. Lora suggested that Sally might try doing some of the exercises that had been previously assigned, but this, like everything else, fell on deaf ears.

Friday morning—the day the ambulance was scheduled to deliver Sally to the rehabilitation unit—proved to be as bad as Lora had feared. Sally woke up "sick," and demanded that the arrangements be canceled. Elizabeth was in tears as she bathed Sally, washed her hair, and put on her the pink kitten-decorated sweatsuit.

Sally claimed that if she ate anything she'd throw up, and Elizabeth said the same was true for her, so Lora ate the breakfast she'd prepared for her sister. Lora was the one to open the door for the emergency medical technician and volunteer fire fighter who manned the ambulance.

They must be used to uncooperative patients for, with teasing and capable handling, they got Sally onto the gurney and away from the house in surprisingly short order. Elizabeth walked beside her once they'd maneuvered the ramp, but Sally neither looked at nor spoke to her mother. Elizabeth's promise, "Lora and I will come visit this evening," was not acknowledged.

The driver smiled and patted Elizabeth on the arm as he went around to open his door. "Don't worry, ma'am. Lots of patients are like this when they're taken someplace they don't want to go. It'll get better. Honest."

Even though she'd agreed that this was for the best, Elizabeth was now filled with guilt and recrimination. There must have been something more she and Lora could have done to help Sally at home.

Lora went outside and did some trimming around the trees then pulled weeds that had grown up beside the back steps. She was sure that what had been done was right, but it was still painful to have her family against her.

She thought of phoning Michael, knowing he'd give support, but she didn't let herself make the call. This was a workday and he was a busy man. She had no right to bother him at his office. He'd offered to come this morning and be here when the ambulance arrived for Sally, but she'd felt this would be an imposition.

At eleven-thirty she went inside and invited her mother to lunch at a nearby steak house. "I can't remember the two of us going out together for a meal in the last ten years," she added.

Elizabeth's eyes were red from crying and at first she wanted to stay home. Finally she said, "I guess it is time we go," and went to her room to change her clothing and put on makeup.

They both tried to keep the conversation upbeat during the meal and Lora knew this must be as hard for Mom as for her. Sally was not mentioned then or after they returned. Lora stripped the electric bed and started doing laundry while her mother headed for the kitchen saying, "I've been wanting to clean the stove and this is as good a time as any."

Their evening meal was light. Their drive to rehab was almost silent. Their reception was frigid. Their visit was brief.

Michael had tried calling Lora at noon, again when he guessed they'd be eating their evening meal, and also later. By the time he had the children in bed, he was pacing the floor.

His mother looked up from the newspaper. "It's all right with me if you'd like to leave, Michael. The little ones are asleep and I'm planning on nothing more taxing than turning pages or clicking the remote control."

He turned to face her. "I'm not hard to read, am I?"

"Not tonight you aren't." He'd told her how stressful this day must be for Lora. "Go to her, son. She needs you more than we do right now."

He bent to kiss her on the cheek. "Thanks, Mom."

She stopped him as he was almost to the door. "I baked an extra peach pie this afternoon. Want to take it along?"

"Sounds like a great idea!" Transporting it carefully, he arrived at the Donnavan home twenty minutes later.

Lora opened the door, drew him inside, and threw her arms around him. "Oh, Michael, I'm so glad you came."

Holding the pie with one hand, he hugged her closely with the other arm. He made no effort to release himself from her embrace, her kisses. Finally, when they were standing cheek against cheek, he rumpled her curls and murmured, "I'm coming over more often if this is the reception I get."

She still clung to him and he knew her trembling was more than excitement at his presence. "What is it, Lora?"

She led him into the area to the right of the hallway, across from Sally's room. He'd never been in this little-used room with its semiformal marble and walnut fire-place, Ethan Allen furniture, and highly polished baby grand piano.

She didn't even notice the pie until she was about to seat herself on the early American sofa. He explained that his mother had baked and sent it and by the time Lora expressed her gratitude and was assured he'd prefer waiting till later to eat some of it, she seemed more herself.

He ached for her as she told how miserable her day had been and that she'd felt so alone in making the necessary decisions and carrying them out. "Why didn't you call me?"

She looked down at her hand held by his. "I wanted to," she confessed, "but I know how busy you are. . . ."

How could he make her understand? "You still can't believe you don't have to carry all your burdens alone," he said. "Don't you know I was praying for you this entire day? I would have welcomed the opportunity of being with you."

"I did know that," she said. "It's probably how I got through even as well as I did." Her gaze came upward to meet his. "And, yes, I was praying, too. For strength and courage and wisdom for all of us."

Her mother, wearing a lightweight robe, came down the hall from her bedroom and all of them were soon seated around the kitchen table with cups of tea and large pieces of thick, juicy pie. Mrs. Donnavan immediately started telling him in detail how "poor Sally" hated to leave and that "there are no promises as to how much better she can get."

He tried to encourage by reminding her of what he'd been told concerning the interview with the doctor, but this made little difference. He realized how drained Lora was by the persistent negativism.

Mrs. Donnavan showed no sign of giving them time alone and he finally said he'd be going. Lora walked him to his car but didn't get in even when he suggested it. He didn't want to leave her like this.

He remembered her nightmares and asked if she were more apt to have them when under this kind of pressure or exhaustion. She admitted they were more likely then, but said she'd had none for the last couple of weeks. When he asked if it might help if he stayed here for the night—there on the couch, while she was in her own room—she sent him home.

Yet in a way it no longer seemed like home when she was not there with him. He tried to sleep but could not. He paced the floor and worried. Then he began to pray. *Dear God, please let Lora sleep through the night and keep her free of bad dreams. Help her to be able to not only accept but to ask for the help and love both You and*

I so want to share with her. Give her peace. . . . He finally fell asleep in his recliner while reading Psalms.

He awoke to unidentifiable sounds that returning consciousness translated into whispers. "Do you s'pose we can wake him?" Chuck was asking.

"Grandma says we shouldn't," Abbie answered. "But I wonder why he slept down here instead of in his bed."

He opened his eyes and smiled at them. He opened his arms and drew them to him. All at once he had such an urge to cry that he had to do something totally physical. Tucking one of them under each arm, he ran toward the kitchen. "Let's have breakfast. I'm starved."

He got out the frying pan, eggs, and cheese and whipped up an omelet. Abbie poured orange juice, even for her father this morning, and only spilled a few drops. Chuck got silverware from the drawer and carefully placed knives and spoons on the right side of the plates and forks on folded napkins on the left.

Their grandmother came, giving proper appreciation for the delicious breakfast, but was not allowed to even put bread in the toaster, for Abbie had asked for that privilege.

Still, Michael could not get his thoughts completely on things here. Over in Belpark was the woman he loved, the woman he longed to make his wife. He did not wish to wake anyone in that household, but he wondered how Lora was. How soon could he call? How long could he stand not phoning?

There was a knock at the front door. It was strange to hear a knock instead of the ringing of the bell and, glancing from the window, he saw the golden Nissan at the end of his front walk. He hurried to welcome Lora.

She was smiling, but she didn't hold out her arms to him. Instead, she remained where she was, on his doorstep, her hands tightly gripping a small tote bag.

He reached for her, but she shook her head. "Before you even wish me a good morning, Michael, I have a question for you, a favor to ask. Is that all right?"

Nothing would feel quite right until she was in his arms, but he nodded. "All right, dear."

Her smile matched the brilliance of the summer sun. "Michael, my beloved, whom I trust completely, would you please teach me to swim?"

She reached into the bag and started to pull out her blue swimsuit. Suddenly she was in his arms, and he knew that his prayers were answered.

Lora, too, was home.

A Letter To Our Readers

Dear Reader:

In order that we might better contribute to your reading enjoyment, we would appreciate your taking a few minutes to respond to the following questions and return to:

Karen Carroll, Editor
Heartsong Presents
P.O. Box 719
Uhrichsville, Ohio 44683

1. Did you enjoy reading *Escort Homeward*?
   ❑ Very much. I would like to see more books by this author!
   ❑ Moderately
   ❑ I would have enjoyed it more if

   _____

2. Where did you purchase this book?_____

   _____

3. What influenced your decision to purchase this book?
   ❑ Cover   ❑ Back cover copy
   ❑ Title   ❑ Friends
   ❑ Publicity   ❑ Other _____

4. Please rate the following elements from 1 (poor) to 10 (superior).
   - ☐ Heroine   ☐ Plot
   - ☐ Hero   ☐ Inspirational theme
   - ☐ Setting   ☐ Secondary characters

5. What settings would you like to see in Heartsong Presents Books?

   _____

   _____

6. What are some inspirational themes you would like to see treated in future books?

   _____

   _____

7. Would you be interested in reading other Heartsong Presents Books?
   - ☐ Very interested
   - ☐ Moderately interested
   - ☐ Not interested

8. Please indicate your age range:
   - ☐ Under 18   ☐ 25-34   ☐ 46-55
   - ☐ 18-24   ☐ 35-45   ☐ Over 55

Name _____

Occupation _____

Address _____

City _____ State _____ Zip _____

HEARTS♥NG PRESENTS books are inspirational romances in contemporary and historical settings, designed to give you an enjoyable, spirit-lifting reading experience.

LOVE A GREAT LOVE STORY?

Introducing Heartsong Presents —
Your Inspirational Book Club

Heartsong Presents Christian romance reader's service will provide you with four never before published romance titles each month! In fact, your books will be mailed to you at the same time advance copies are sent to book reviewers. You'll preview each of these new and unabridged books before they are released to the general public.

These books are filled with the kind of stories you have been longing for—stories of courtship, chivalry, honor, and virtue. Strong characters and riveting plot lines will make you want to read on and on. Romance is not dead, and each of these romantic tales will remind you that Christian faith is still the vital ingredient in an intimate relationship filled with true love and honest devotion.

Sign up today to receive your first set. Send no money now. We'll bill you only $9.97 post-paid with your shipment. Then every month you'll automatically receive the latest four "hot off the press" titles for the same low post-paid price of $9.97. That's a savings of 50% off the $4.95 cover price. When you consider the exaggerated shipping charges of other book clubs, your savings are even greater!

THERE IS NO RISK—you may cancel at any time without obligation. And if you aren't completely satisfied with any selection, return it for an immediate refund.

TO JOIN, just complete the coupon below, mail it today, and get ready for hours of wholesome entertainment every month.

Now you can curl up, relax, and enjoy some great reading full of the warmhearted spirit of romance.